Miles Gibson

was born in 1947. He spent his childhood in a wet and draughty seaside town on the edge of the New Forest, and now lives and works in London. The first of his highly-acclaimed novels was published in 1984 and translated into several languages. His other work includes a collection of short stories and a book of poems for children.

D1152307

Other books by Miles Gibson
published by The Do-Not Press

THE SANDMAN
DANCING WITH MERMAIDS
VINEGAR SOUP

Kingdom Swann

The Story of a Photographer

MILES GIBSON

This edition published in Great Britain in 1998 by
The Do-Not Press
PO Box 4215
London SE23 2QD

First Published in Great Britain in 1990
by William Heinemann Ltd

Front jacket photograph from the Retrograph Archive, London.

ISBN 1 899344 34 9

British Library Cataloguing in Publication Data. A catalogue
record for this book is available from the British Library.

h g f e d c b a

Printed and bound in Great Britain by The Guernsey Press Co Ltd.

Front cover picture courtesy of the Retrograph Archive, London

In memory of Kingdon Swann
1825-1916

"Tis the times plague, when madmen lead the blind.'

The Earl of Gloucester
King Lear, Act IV

1

'Women will be the death of me,' mutters Kingdom Swann, whistling through his whiskers. He is a large, impressive, old man with a wonderful wealth of beard. He wears a black frock-coat, unbuttoned to show a velvet waistcoat and a pair of nankeen pantaloons. At his throat he sports a necktie of crimson silk and his head is warmed by a Turkish skull-cap embellished with beads and silver threads.

'Women will be the death of me.'

He looks up at the fat, nude woman hung by her wrists from a pillar. She wears nothing but iron chains. She has neat breasts, plump arms and heavy, fully fashioned thighs that hide a voluptuous nest of curls. Her face is flushed with rouge and flowers wilt in her tangled hair.

'Are you ready, Mr Swann?' she shouts, impatiently shaking her shackles.

Swann grunts, closes one eye and lets the hood fall over his head.

2

He was born in 1825 and trained, at an early age, to be a classical painter. He was accepted as a pupil of the most celebrated artist of the day, Hippolyte Fletcher-Whitby, at his studio in St John's Wood.

The old master was famous for his huge, allegorical paintings featuring tribes of nimble nudes. These canvases were so large that scaffolding had to be built around them during their execution. Each morning Fletcher-Whitby would send his pupils scrambling up the rigging to work among the gods where, balanced on treacherous planks, they rendered thunder clouds by the yard or drew the smoking peaks of Sodom. The old man, nearly blind and crippled with gout, remained on the ground to gild the folds of Salome's skirt or fiddle with a slave-girl's buttocks.

'Don't spare the pigment!' he would roar as his students daubed at the sky. 'Give me more thunder!'

The young Swann was quickly promoted down the ladder, from backgrounds to foregrounds, and finally given command of the concubines at *The Persians Feast in Babylon*.

By the time of the grand master's death in 1849, Swann had already rented a studio in Piccadilly and settled down to the serious business of making money. He saw no future in Whitby's painted hippodromes and turned his attentions, instead, to picking pockets by painting portraits. For a few guineas he lent chemists, clerics and city drapers all the majesty of Roman generals. He turned their wives into seraphim and pictured their children as cherubs. At the flick of his wrist he could turn grocers into gladiators and matrons into dimpled moppets.

Yet, despite these beneficent talents, he was powerless against photography. In the camera craze that followed the

Great Exhibition he saw the portrait business collapse. For several years he scratched a living by colouring photographs for the camera studios that flourished the length of Regent Street. He submitted landscapes to summer shows and waited for fashions to change. But the great days were gone. When he married a dentist's daughter in 1873 he had already burned his brushes and bought a brass and mahogany camera.

The studio, with its tall north window, was perfect for this new enterprise and Swann was quick with the modern art. Photography, he discovered, was a marvel of simple arithmetic. A tiny carte-de-visite portrait could be sold for a florin or five shillings the imperial dozen. He manufactured them by the thousand and there seemed no end to the public's demand for these gloomy paper shadows.

It wasn't long before he hired a redundant engraver to help him develop and print his work. The engraver's name was Cromwell Marsh. He was a young man with a freckled face and a slick of ginger hair. He was patient and clever and full of crafty ambition. He brought new ideas to the business and quickly doubled their fortunes.

For a trifling extra expense, and the hire of a suitable costume, clients could take advantage of exotic painted back-cloths and amusing *trompe-l'oeil* effects. Ladies might dress as the Empress of China or sit and swing in a paper moon. The men could captain a submarine or wave their hats from a canvas balloon. These scenes would be cleverly coloured and framed in gilt for a guinea.

When his wife died in the Great Frost of 1895, Kingdom Swann was a wealthy man. He should have retired and spent his few remaining years slumped by the fire with his dreams. At the ripe old age of seventy he was ready to retreat from the world. But the world hadn't finished with Kingdom Swann.

It began with the Rossetti sisters. They had appeared in the shop one afternoon in the summer of 1890. They were hand-some girls with fine complexions and lacquered wreaths of auburn hair. The youngest of the two sisters wore a great deal of lace and a hat embroidered with flowers. The eldest, who was no more than twenty, wore a bird of paradise on her head. They were dainty. They were charming. There was nothing in their general appearance to make the old man suspicious. When they expressed the desire to be photographed, he led them into the studio, explaining all the mechanical illusions they might use to their advantage.

But, despite his best endeavours, the girls were not impressed. The younger Rossetti stifled a yawn. Her sister sighed and looked disappointed. They were hoping, she explained, to create a tableau in which the virtues of photographic naturalism contrived to enhance a more traditional study of antique beauty.

Kingdom Swann frowned and played with his albert. The studio was hot. He felt his collar cutting his neck.

'A study in which a brief invocation to Aphrodite might be caught, with absolute fidelity, for the admiration of an intimate circle of friends,' suggested the younger sister.

Swann felt distinctly uncomfortable.

'May we trust in your discretion, Mr Swann?' enquired the elder.

'Have we made ourselves understood?'

Swann blew thoughtfully through his beard. He looked at the ceiling. He shuffled his shoes. He nodded. Yes. He understood. As a prayer to Psyche, in the cause of art and natural beauty, in honour of everything high and mighty, they wanted to show him their bums.

The Rossetti sisters looked pleased with themselves. After some hesitation the elder Rossetti opened a bag and pulled out a little, morocco album. The album was entirely the work of Miss Alice Chinn, a photographer famous for her female studies. Swann took the book and modestly peeked at its pages.

Here was Lady Woodbine Fitzherbert, stripped to her slippers and shamelessly sporting a fine, black tuft as she danced in *The Dream of Pygmalion*. Here was Miss Hester Pontefract, big as a walrus, diddeys let dangle, engaged in *The Ritual Toilet of Venus*. There were twenty or more such photographs featuring grand and expensive women and each nude study, no matter how lewd, was granted a classical epithet. A fine, plump woman wearing nought but a necklace had been blessed with *The Charm of Europa*. A right royal strumpet exposing her buttocks had been graced with *The Shame of Lucretia*.

Swann spent no longer than he dared reviewing the naked charms of London's high society. He knew such albums were the height of fashion but, none the less, it was work for the lady photographers. He couldn't understand why these handsome sisters wanted him to inspect their mutton.

'Miss Chinn is a very accomplished photographer,' he said, trying to return the album. 'No one could hope to serve you with more grace and understanding.'

This observation had the most unfortunate effect on the younger Rossetti who promptly burst into tears. Swann was bewildered.

'Poor Miss Chinn has only lately met with a terrible accident,' confided the elder Rossetti as they helped her sister into a chair. 'A runaway horse in the Charing Cross Road...' She fluttered her hand. The bird of paradise ruffled its feathers. Swann made sympathetic noises and hurried to fetch a glass of seltzer.

'She always thought highly of your works, Mr Swann,' sobbed the younger Rossetti when she found the strength to speak again. 'She spoke of you as a true artist.' She turned her lovely dark eyes to heaven. The hat had wilted. Her tears left pink stains on the perfectly rice-powdered face.

'But when we learned that you had studied under the famous Fletcher-Whitby...' continued the elder with a sudden flush of excitement.

'The *great* Fletcher-Whitby,' her sister said as she wiped her nose.

'The modern Michelangelo,' declared the elder, nodding her head.

'We had do doubt that you were our man.'

'No doubt.'

'Quite so.'

'And since the album is not yet complete,' announced the elder breathlessly, 'we place ourselves confidently in your hands.'

And so, the next afternoon, the sisters shed their corsets, button boots and stockings to be artfully transformed into *Concubines of Babylon*. They were so absorbed in their silly charade that they soon forgot their modesty, letting Swann lead them on to the stage and chain their wrists to a plaster pillar.

The old man spent a long time arranging their limbs and gently pulling the pins from their hair. They didn't seem in the least disturbed by the work of his preening fingers. Wrapped in nothing but their own conceits they patiently hung from the chains and practised expressions of wistful surrender.

When Swann was happy with the effect he retired to peep through the camera. It was an old-fashioned tailboard Winchester and he stood, hypnotised with pleasure, his head wrapped up in a black cotton cloth, admiring the charms of his prisoners.

It wasn't until the light failed, with the plates finished and the sisters no more than silhouettes, that he felt obliged to set them free. As soon as the chains fell away, as if released from a narcolepsy, they cried out and shivered and looked confused. At once the young Rossetti, in a state of terrible agitation, shrank from Swann's touch and tried to cover her breasts with her hands. The elder sister turned her back when he tried to help her from the stage and tartly dimpled her buttocks. The spell had been broken. In a minute or two they were dressed for the street and buttoned through to the throat. They looked so demure in their frocks and hats. No one would guess they had ever been his fat and tempting concubines. They thanked him for his trouble and paid him into the bargain. They collected their purchase the following day and he never heard from them again.

3

It was Cromwell Marsh who saw the opportunity. He kept his eyes open. He knew the wicked way of the world. And the world wanted filthy photographs. There were, to his certain knowledge, a dozen bookshops on the Strand that had nothing to sell but grossly indecent keyhole snaps. He had recently purchased, for his own amusement, a set of German postcards that were admirably obscene. It was only a question of convincing Swann that his last great work should be *The Torment of Tantalus*.

The more he thought about it, the better he liked it, until one evening in a Soho saloon, he explained the scheme to his aged employer. He didn't approach the subject at once, but made the photographer comfortable with several bottles of Reids' strong stout and encouraged him to talk of the past. He watched as Swann puffed out with pride to remember himself as a painter. He listened to accounts of long-forgotten Royal Academy exhibitions, threats against the Impressionist smudgers and praise for the talents of Fletcher-Whitby.

'I can remember when Whitby finished his masterpiece,' dreamed Swann. 'I think it must have been '47. *A Vandal Spoiling Roman Women*.'

'That must have been a sight,' said Cromwell Marsh, to encourage him. He lit a paper cigar and blew a smoke ring into the air.

Swann shone. 'They stood for six hours in the rain for a chance to admire that canvas,' he said. 'It won medals. They had to use troops to control the crowds.'

Cromwell Marsh sighed and shook his head. 'Those days are gone,' he said mournfully.

The truth of this remark nearly crushed the old man. His face shrank on the bone, his flesh turned grey, his mouth decayed and the tufts of his eyebrows quivered. He suddenly shrivelled under his clothes, sagged and sank, until his very life seemed threatened. 'These days it's nothing but bicycles,' he muttered. He had a morbid dread of bicycles, especially those with pneumatic tyres. They came spinning from nowhere, hiding in the horses' legs, striking at you from every direction, terrible, swift and silent as death. 'You can't paint bicycles,' he complained. 'You couldn't have painted the Duke of Wellington sitting on a bicycle.'

'It's a bugger,' said Marsh.

Swann stared around the saloon, searching the legs of the crowd for the blood-stained breeches of a vulcanite assassin. The glare of the gas mantles hurt his eyes. 'What's happening to the world,' he grieved, trying to pull himself together. '*A Vandal Spoiling Roman Women*. These days a man wouldn't give you tuppence.'

'I was thinking,' said Marsh. 'I was thinking we might play some part in the public edification.' He paused and leaned forward in his chair. 'A selection of unwrapped classical beauties,' he continued, in a confidential tone of voice, 'presented for the pleasure of the common man.'

'Unwrapped beauties?'

'Fine works of art brought to life with the camera.'

'Photographs?' growled Swann suspiciously.

'Special photographs. *Harlots of the Turkish Harem. Vandals Spoiling Roman Women*.'

'There's no art in photography,' said Swann.

Cromwell Marsh shrugged and sipped at his beer. 'I heard that Delacroix painted direct from the photograph,' he said mildly.

'I don't believe it!' roared Swann.

'It's true,' returned Marsh. 'They found the albums after his death. Dozens of 'em. He never painted a man or woman that wasn't first posed in a photograph.'

Swann looked appalled. 'He was a Frenchie,' he said at last, as if that were the only explanation.

'But he was an artist,' said Cromwell Marsh. 'He was an artist and no mistake.'

'That's a matter of opinion, sir.'

'And don't forget the Pre-Raphaelites,' said Marsh. 'They soon took to the photograph.'

'Wicked rumours!' exploded Swann. 'Rumours and filthy gossip!' He adored the work of the Brotherhood and would have nothing said against them.

'I'm not saying they copied direct from the camera,' corrected Marsh, 'but old John Ruskin, rest his soul, used to think it a most convenient method of collecting studies of figures and costumes...'

'Sketches from life,' blustered Swann. 'Fletcher-Whitby used pattern books. He kept hundreds of different mountains and trees.'

'That's the idea,' said Marsh. 'And if the painter trusts the *camera's* eye,' he continued slowly, 'think what the camera might accomplish should it borrow the *painter's* vision.'

'What?' demanded Swann, beginning to grow obstreperous.

'Everything!' laughed Marsh. 'Paper prints into naturalist art, life into dreams, men and women into gods!' He sat back and stared at the ceiling. A smile spread across his freckled face as he watched the phantasmagoria in the smoke of his paper cigar.

'Why?' Swann sieved stout through his big moustache. 'Where's the rhyme and reason to it?'

'Reason?' echoed Marsh. He looked at his companion in surprise. 'Why, they'll call it the new crusade for beauty. By the time we've finished every man will own a work of art, at a price he can afford, to study in the comfort of his own home.'

'A very pretty speech,' said Swann. 'But I don't believe it.'

'Correct,' said Marsh. 'Quite correct. And I'd agree with you if we was talking about Mr Nobody-in-Particular. It couldn't be done by anyone. You'd need a proper painter from the old school to understand it.'

'It's a waste of time,' insisted Swann. 'They don't want real works of art any more. These days it's peepshows and waxworks.'

'You've got to move with the times,' argued Marsh. 'Remember the Rossetti sisters.'

'Who?' frowned Swann.

'Concubines,' said Marsh. 'They was *Concubines of Babylon*.'

'We can't sell *them* to the *hoi polloi*,' protested the baffled Swann.

'Similar,' said Marsh, who had secretly printed and sold the sisters at least a dozen times.

'How?'

'I'll show you.'

'I'm waiting,' said Swann.

Cromwell Marsh wasted no time. He recruited models from the choicest brothels in Covent Garden. He built scenery, invented costumes and propped Swann behind the Winchester. It was simple.

When whores dropped their drawers Swann saw *The Daughters of Titan*. He didn't know that his Aphrodite was later sold as a Willing Wagtail. He didn't ask questions. His days were a grand parade of strutting, naked strumpets. They came in every size and shape and were skilfully portrayed as nymphs and mermaids, sylphs and sprites, in scenes of gross indecency.

Marsh sold the work, under the counter, as a series of popular novelties generally known as Gentlemen's Relish. For the sum of five guineas, he wrote in the catalogue, the curious may marvel at the lubricity of plump, young beauties, surprised in their most voluptuous moments, providing such a feast for the eye that nothing shall be left to the imagination.

4

It was on the 12th March 1902 that they first received word from Lord Hugo Prattle. His lordship, exhausting the catalogue, wanted *Jezebel in French Lace Drawers*. He wrote to Swann on a sheet of gold-flecked paper, begging him to accept the commission.

'Prattle!' crooned Marsh as he read the letter to his master. 'The compliments of Lord Hugo Prattle.'

'I never heard of him,' said Swann.

'I am surprised,' said Marsh. 'Lord Hugo Prattle is the biggest collector in Europe. He collects photographs like any other man might take to collecting etchings or books. They say he's gathered a million studies expressing the undraped female form and shows 'em off in a private museum. They say he's found examples of every race and colour on earth. Some of 'em are very rare species. He's famous for it. Why, if he likes your work we'll be famous ourselves. It's like an appointment to royalty.'

'The Queen, God rest her soul, was fond of collecting photographs,' said Swann.

'It's a noble pursuit,' said Marsh.

Swann frowned. 'But I can't imagine Jezebel corrupting the land of Israel in a pair of French lace drawers.'

Marsh opened his mouth and closed it again. The old man had a knack of asking difficult questions. 'It's the modern interpretation,' he said at last, scratching his chin.

'Is that right?' said Swann.

'No doubt about it,' said Marsh, studying his fingernails. 'You're supposed to think of the fancy drawers as a mark of Phoenician decadence.'

They chose a model called Alice Hancock for this important

work. She was a large and classical beauty who liked to surround herself with scandal. It was rumoured she had once been mounted by the young Prince of Wales who had paid for the pleasure by filling her purse with pearls. No one knew the truth of it. She was certainly a handsome woman and because of her biblical proportions found regular work in front of the camera. She was fond of the old man and proud to flaunt her mutton.

It was a cold, rain-sodden afternoon when she arrived at the Piccadilly studio. Her boots were so wet and her hands so cold that Marsh had to fill her with gin before she agreed to take off her clothes.

'You call these drawers?' she demanded when they gave her the costume. She held the confection against the light and hooted with derision. It was a curious little skirt hung with clusters of pink ribbon roses and divided with buttons made from mother-of-pearl.

'They're only for decoration,' said Marsh impatiently. 'They're just to gild your lily.'

'They're symbolic,' said Swann helpfully. He began absently slapping his pockets, in search of the aniseed balls he sucked for his concentration.

Alice looked sceptical but she was too cold to argue with them. She forced her buttocks into the knickers and climbed aboard a pedestal that was bolted securely into the stage. She had rouged her nipples and braided her hair. She held a spear in her hands.

'A picture!' said Marsh, as he stepped back to admire the effect. He raised a hand to his face and squinted through a crack in his fingers.

Swann crouched at the camera and managed, by chance, to expose a plate. 'There is nothing so remarkable as the loveliness of women,' he said, clicking an aniseed ball against his teeth.

Alice grunted and tilted her head. 'Have you finished?' she said. She was trying to keep an eye on her boots that were starting to steam beside the stove. They were nearly new and she didn't want them spoiled.

'A fine performance,' said Marsh. 'A stimulating composition. But, none the less, I think we should take the posterior view to avoid any disappointment.'

So Alice turned, very gingerly, and thrust out her copious rump. 'How's that?' she called.

'I never saw such a Jezebel!' grinned Marsh.

The drawers protested and burst their buttons.

'Can you smell burning?' Swann said suddenly, pulling his face from the camera.

Alice shrieked, swung on her heels and toppled from the pedestal. She plunged forward with her arms outstretched and knocked Kingdom Swann to the floor. She was bruised and dusty and frightened. She sat on Swann's face and howled.

'Quick!' shouted Marsh. 'He's suffocating!' He stared in horror as Swann gave a feeble kick and clawed at the mighty flanks with his hands. But Alice was too shocked to understand. It was left to Marsh to prise her open at the knees and fight to save the photographer. He delivered Swann's head and was trying to drag him out by the ears before Alice recovered her wits.

'Is he dead?' she moaned, lifting her weight from the artist's body. She was still clutching her spear.

Marsh frowned and squeezed Swann's wrist. 'I don't know,' he muttered anxiously. 'The shock alone was enough to kill him.'

'He's too old for this game,' said Alice. 'The poor old sod should be home in bed with a good fire and an egg custard. I shouldn't wonder if I broke his bones.'

'No!' cried Marsh in great alarm. 'He's an artist. He's an old master. There aren't so many left surviving. What will happen when he's gone?'

'You'll think of something,' said Alice.

'He was like a father to me,' sobbed Marsh.

They knelt together in prayer and stared at the silent face.

'Look, he's breathing again!' shouted Alice, at last, as Swann stirred enough to open his eyes.

'Thank the Lord!' exclaimed Marsh. 'I thought for a minute we'd lost him.' He took Swann by the sleeves and gently hauled him to his feet.

Alice flung her arms around the old man and covered him in kisses. 'Are you hurt?' she murmured. 'Shall we fetch a doctor?'

Swann staggered into a chair and nursed his nose in his hands. His face burned. His beard had been split and wonderfully spiced. He pulled on his nose and peered around him. He was confused. What was happening here? He glanced doubtfully at the big, nude woman, sucked on his whiskers and sneezed.

'No harm done,' blushed Alice and hoicked at the French lace drawers.

5

The pains Swann had taken with Jezebel did not go unre-warded.

Lord Hugo Prattle was so pleased with his purchase that he called a few months later to discuss a more ambitious venture. He was a short man with a big belly and a whiskered face. He carried an old-fashioned cut to his clothes and despite the fine weather wore a silk plush hat and an overcoat with a wilting buttonhole. He marched into the shop, doffed his topper and shook Cromwell Marsh by the hand. Marsh directed him through the studio and introduced the proprietor.

It was his intention to commission *The Rape of the Sabine Women in Fifty Stereoscopic Views* and to feature himself as Romulus. The Swann Studio would recruit the Sabines from all the better London brothels. Fifty, female, all different, clean and healthy, pink and plump, no Irish, must be Christian. During the work, which he trusted would last no more than ten weeks, he would stay at his club. He would arrive at the studio each afternoon at three o'clock sharp. A fresh Sabine must be ready and waiting for his immediate attention. During the battle several plates would be exposed from which he would choose the one by which he wished to commemorate the conflict.

'And might we be acquainted with those features thought to be most desirable in a Sabine woman?' enquired Cromwell Marsh.

'Tight titties. Heavy haunches. Large feet.'

'The most noble proportions,' toadied Marsh. 'And might we humbly request the nature of the costumes to be worn as might heighten the effect?'

'Romulus? Helmet with plenty of plume. Gloves for the ladies. Nothing more. Most particular.' He smiled by grinding his teeth. The conversation and the warmth of his surroundings had worked him into a stupendous sweat. He felt forced to sit and open his coat.

Kingdom Swann, too shocked to speak, found a notebook and pencil and scribbled down the order with the diligence of a good head waiter.

'And the campaign fund?' wheedled Marsh. 'Might we beg leave to be informed of his lordship's view to the cost of his military manoeuvres?'

'No idea. Leave it to you.'

'Rest in our prudence,' slubbered Marsh. 'And the engagement. When would his lordship find it most convenient to mount his first conquest?'

'War declared!' honked Lord Hugo Prattle. 'Immediate effect.'

It was the first week of June. London was celebrating the end of the war with the Boers and looking forward to King Edward's coronation. The dusty streets were stuffed with bunting and flags flew from the rooftops. A triumphal arch had been built in Whitehall. The Empire theatre staged a special, patriotic production.

Each morning, after breakfast, Kingdom Swann stepped from his house near Golden Square and walked into Piccadilly, enjoying the noise and the crush of the crowd. So much cavorting! So many young women in the world! And it seemed to him, walking in that sooty sunlight, as if all the beauties who bustled around might, at any time, be summoned by Marsh and sweetly unfrocked in the studio. Who knew how many of them had already had their buttocks blessed by the Winchester? He had grown to be the devil's magician, painting with nothing but sunlight. At the flick of his wrist he turned maids into nymphs fit for Alma-Tadema. He lunched at a chop-house in Cork Street, sitting at a corner table with a pie and a glass of stout. In the afternoon, at three o'clock sharp, he was at the studio to watch his lordship saddle a Sabine. It *was* an art and no mistake. They were days of celebration.

But at night, when the lights blazed and revellers sang in the streets, he returned to the house near Golden Square where Violet Askey, housekeeper, sat in the dark and mourned.

Violet was thirty-four years old, a good-looking woman made narrow and pale with too many years spent standing in shadows. She had lived with Kingdom Swann since the death of his wife in the Great Frost. Having been introduced to the household through such a tragic circumstance she had felt obliged to make a career of mourning. She wore a dress of strong black cotton and her skirts, when she moved, seemed to spread the shadows from room to room. Her hair was black, her eyes were black and the only colour about her face was her nose which was pink and slightly damp as if she were constantly having the vapours. She was a queer and solitary creature and, although she could come and go as she pleased, she rarely ventured beyond the house.

Swann had grown fond of this dismal nurse. When his wife had been alive the place had been full of servants. At night the attic was stuffed to the rafters. But when he looked now at his neighbours, with their jabbering colonies of parlour maids and kitchen boys, he pitied them. So much noise and commotion! An old man needed no such attention. He ate little, said nothing, raised no dust in the cushions and carpets. He was thankful for Violet Askey. He came home each night to silence, sat down in the gloom and let her serve him pork and potatoes.

Two days before the great coronation the King was struck down with perityphlitis and his life was said to hang in the balance. The ceremony was cancelled but the celebrations continued. It seemed a pity to waste the beer. When the King was finally crowned, in August, his subjects were tired but not defeated. They lined the streets to watch the procession, waving little paper flags and roaring their approval. While, not far away, in Piccadilly Lord Hugo Prattle, short of wind and out of pocket, grinding his teeth in pain and pleasure, with his battered helmet moulting feathers, to shouts of encouragement from Marsh, managed to mount his fiftieth Sabine and fell to the ground, exhausted.

6

'They enjoy it,' growled Swann defiantly.

It was Christmas. The walls held wreaths of burnished holly. A goose dinner grew cold upon the table. The coals in the grate gave nothing but smoke.

'No doubt,' said Violet Askey. 'No doubt they enjoy it as well as any woman might endure the invasion of her person if there's pleasure to be found in humiliation.'

'It's harmless enough.'

'Harmless,' echoed Violet, nodding her head. 'Innocent as milk. Driving men to behave like beasts, dragging women to despair, destroying home and family.'

She was wearing one of her best black gowns, a crumbling crinoline embroidered with swags of faded roses. The gown was too large for her shoulders and drooped forlornly at the throat. It smelt of exhausted lavender.

Kingdom Swann stared balefully down at the postcard propped against his plate. It was a lewd view of a fat girl wearing silk stockings and a straw hat. The name of the Swann Studio, Piccadilly, had been artfully embossed, in gold, upon its lower margin.

The local cheesemonger's wife had found the picture hidden in her husband's wardrobe. She had cuffed the husband, removed the card and sent it over to Violet Askey, together with her compliments and a pound of Cheddar. Since the house-keeper had always believed that her master made money by taking portraits of grocers and parsons, the sight of this fat and friendly nude had come as a rude awakening. Her anger, fermented with hot fruit punch, erupted now into fury.

'I take photographs,' said Swann gently, struggling to explain. 'It doesn't hurt them. They earn good money. They get a cup of tea and a slice of cake. They're the finest set of young ladies you're ever likely to meet.'

'God preserve me from the sight of them!' cried Violet, giving the postcard a furtive glance. 'We're living in strange times when honest, Christian Englishwomen go out parading their sacred parts for a cup of tea and a slice of cake!'

'It's honest work.'

'It's the work of the devil!'

'I suppose you have some experience!' shouted Swann impatiently and jumped from his chair. His boots squeaked as he paced the room.

'I can imagine,' shuddered Violet, standing at the table. She continued to stir the great bowl of punch, banging the bobbing fruit with a spoon as if she were drowning kittens. Her long dark hair, so carefully combed and pinned in a cushion, began to unravel around her ears.

'All the work is very artistic,' insisted Swann. 'One of the girls sat for Singer Sargent and he's a man who is most particular. There's nothing unwholesome about it.'

'No more than picnics at the Paris morgue,' conceded Violet. It was a disgrace. She would never feel safe in her bed again. A man his age and poor Mrs Swann so long in her grave. He was a monster. A wicked old fiend feasting on youth and innocence. It gave her the shivers to think what else might be lurking in the tripe of his brain.

'I don't have to answer to you!' roared Swann, although it seemed that he couldn't avoid it.

'No,' said Violet, banging apples. 'But one day you'll answer to God-on-High.'

'What?'

'Yes!' cried Violet triumphantly. 'God who made both men and women and made them in His own likeness.'

'I picture 'em the way He makes 'em: big and bountiful. They're as natural as any other view of nature,' he argued, bending down to poke at the fire. 'Is it wrong to take pleasure in God's own creation?'

'No,' said Violet.

'Is it wrong that God's glory is found reflected in the form of a woman?' said Swann. 'Is God wrong?'

'No,' said Violet, stamping her foot.

'And are the paintings of Singer Sargent wrong? Is it wrong for a man to paint what he finds most divine in the world?'

Violet had never seen the paintings of Singer Sargent although she didn't care for such a military name. 'It's altogether different,' she said, gulping at a glass of punch. 'A true artist would never want to portray a woman wearing nothing but stockings and a sailor straw!'

'It's the fashion.'

Violet snorted and refilled her glass. 'It's a queer fashion when Art parades without her drawers.'

'Photography is the modern art,' argued Swann. 'It's a magic mirror. The only reliable method of turning life into art.'

'Nonsense! How can art be so gross and *hairy*? It's not natural.'

'Life is hairy!' shouted Kingdom Swann, storming about the room and making the holly wreaths tremble.

'We're talking about art,' returned Violet, clutching the edge of the tablecloth. 'Art has never been hairy. The Greeks and Romans were never hairy. I'd be obliged if you can find me a hairy Rubens. It's not natural.'

'Yes,' insisted the photographer. 'Don't you see? It's natural to life. That's the beauty of it.' He remembered what Cromwell Marsh had said about the Swann crusade for enlightenment. A world in which every man might own a work of art, at a price he could afford, to enjoy in the comfort of his own home.

'If life is beauty, where's the reason to art?' said Violet, thoroughly confused.

'Art is a celebration of life!' cried Swann. 'Why, with a little patience and a clear eye, you'll find more beauty in a scullery-maid than all the statues of ancient Rome. Bring me a girl with some fat on her bone and I'll show you Helen of Troy.'

'Shame on you!' gasped the blushing Violet.

'Bless my soul,' declared Swann. 'But you're quite enough of a beauty yourself.' He turned upon the trembling woman, thrust out his beard and surveyed her with a professional eye. 'I'd like to see you with your hair combed out and a pinch of colour in your cheeks. You'd make a dish fit for kings.'

'Stop or I'll scream,' groaned Violet.

'There's no shame in it,' said Swann. He stepped forward and stretched out his hand, hoping to tilt her head to the light.

This was too much for Violet Askey. She raised her fist and threatened him with the ladle. 'You're a wicked, wicked man, Kingdom Swann!' And she fainted into his arms.

It was a very difficult Christmas.

7

The housekeeper wouldn't talk to him. It was her New Year's resolution. She managed the house and conducted all her domestic affairs as if he had suddenly ceased to exist. She no longer came to clean his room or sweep the ashes from the grate. He washed in cold water, ate cold food and found his laundry neglected. Kingdom Swann was furious. It was no weather for monkey business. But when he challenged Violet she burst into tears and locked herself in the scullery.

'She's ignoring me!' he complained to Marsh. 'There should be a law against it.'

'You'll find there's laws against everything,' reflected Marsh. 'But it don't stop a man being robbed of his teeth.' He'd had a very difficult week – shown the dentist a rotten molar and had his whole mouth condemned.

'It's natural to lose your teeth,' said Swann. 'I had mine pulled before I was thirty.'

'Times was different,' scowled Marsh.

'Teeth don't change,' said Swann. 'It's not hygienic for a man your age to want to preserve his natural teeth. What can I do about Violet?'

'Give her a dose of Gregory's powder,' said Cromwell Marsh. 'I suspect she's constipated. Have you tried changing her rations? You'll be surprised at the difference it makes.'

'I've tried everything,' said Swann very bitterly. 'I've coaxed her and teased her and threatened her and none of it works. She spends all her time avoiding me.'

'What have you done to upset the girl?' asked Marsh and then grinned to think of his master chasing the housekeeper up and down stairs. There's no fool like an old fool and a man never loses his appetite for a nice fat leg when it's wrapped in a stocking.

'Nothing!' protested Swann.

'Then turn her out on the street,' said Marsh. 'They say the shock helps to clarify their heads. Mrs Marsh – may God preserve that woman's health – has often had cause to turn out the cook. I've known our cook stay out overnight and make up a bed in the garden shed. It's cruel, I'll admit, but it's a lesson that works a miracle on the Saturday beef and dumplings.'

'I didn't know you had trouble with the cook,' said Swann.

'Oh, yes,' said Marsh proudly, as if it were the talk of London. 'She's acquired an uncommon weakness for soldiers. She can't resist the uniform. One or two might be forgiven but the cook don't know when enough is sufficient. They're down in our kitchen, day and night, like flies around a bull's arse. And she feeds 'em from the family larder! That's why Mrs Marsh feels obliged to turn her out of the house.'

'I couldn't turn Violet out of her home,' said Swann. He was shocked at the suggestion. He sometimes worried about Cromwell Marsh. The man had a cruel sense of humour.

'It's a pity,' shrugged Marsh. 'You've the perfect weather for it.'

'The frost at night would slaughter a horse!'

'Correct,' said Marsh. 'The effect is very sobering.'

'No,' said Swann. 'It's not decent. I couldn't bring myself to lock the woman out in the cold.'

'I find that a leather slipper slapped against the posterior has a remarkably warming effect,' murmured Marsh. 'Although, I dare say, it's not to everyone's taste.'

'She used to be such a good-hearted girl,' sighed Swann. 'A trifle sour but always good-hearted.'

'It's her age,' said Marsh. 'It's time that woman was married. She's the last of the bestial virgins.'

'I can't make sense of it,' said Swann. He was reluctant to confess the reason for her bad behaviour since he didn't want Marsh to think of him as a man who could be bullied by the likes of a bad-tempered housekeeper. She ought to know her place and, besides, if he'd worked in oils or watercolours he knew she'd have given her blessing to stuff the studio *full* of nudes and be proud to call him an artist. It was only the thought of the camera that gave the woman the frights.

'Women has strange notions,' said Cromwell Marsh, poking at the holes in his teeth. 'It's the moon. The moon slows the flow of blood to their brains. You can't expect them to think like men when they don't have regular brains. That's why God made 'em ornamental.'

It was a miserable winter. There were days of wicked, slashing winds that knocked down horses, pulled out trees and sucked old women from their shoes. There were nights of penetrating frost that shattered cobbles, turned out graves and petrified the Thames. There were weeks when the city was steeped in fog, the streets filled with ghosts, the studio frozen and too dark for work.

'That's enough or I'll catch me death,' grumbled Gloria Spooner, whenever they tried to remove her vest.

Cromwell Marsh had fetched her from Soho to be a Babylonian Beauty. They wanted her sitting on leopard skins, surrounded by bowls of bright, wax fruit. It had been one of Swann's ideas, based on a little-known canvas by Hippolyte Fletcher-Whitby.

Gloria was a favourite model but suffered badly in the cold. She was a beautiful girl, fat as a firkin, with a strong, Pre-Raphaelite face and a backside dancing with dimples.

'We can't take your picture wearing a vest,' said Marsh as he fiddled with her buttons.

'I'm cold,' she snapped and pushed him away.

'A sailor's life is not always beer, bum and bacca,' scolded Marsh as he hurried back to his chair by the stove. You had to suffer sometimes for art.

'Don't talk so vulgar,' said Gloria.

'Think of the heat of the Holy Land,' said Swann as he blew through his mittens.

'It's hot,' said Marsh. 'The sand burns your feet. It hasn't rained for seven years.'

'You're a pagan queen,' shivered Swann. 'You're sitting alone in a big silk tent, awaiting the pleasures of a tribal king.' He had tried to suggest an Arabian tent by suspending great swags of printed cotton from hooks above the stage. The leopard skins had been hired, at great expense, from a high-class furrier and would have to go back at the end of the day.

'I want to wait in my clothes,' said Gloria stubbornly. She felt so cold that her ears were ringing.

'No,' insisted Cromwell Marsh. 'It's unthinkable! You can't be a pagan queen while you're dressed in that ugly vest.'

'Why?'

'Because this is art!' shouted Marsh. 'And you want to show the king how you're made!' He hooked open the door of the stove and thrashed at the coals with a poker. The stove belched sparks and the fire went out.

'Is he a nice-looking gent?' said Gloria, pulling a leopard skin snugly over her knees.

'An aristocrat,' said Swann confidentially.

'Is he tall?'

'A bloody Goliath!' raged Marsh.

'What colour are his eyes?' demanded Gloria, who was not in the least impressed with his tantrums.

'I don't know! What colour would you like in the eye of a tribal king?' shouted Marsh. He paced up and down in a fury, stamping his feet and beating the air with a poker.

'Blue,' said Gloria.

'All right! He's a king with bright blue eyes and you're waiting for his pleasure. And when he arrives I hope he gives you a damn good whipping!'

'He'll have to wait,' growled Gloria, reaching for her hat and coat. 'It's cold enough to freeze me vitals.' She had a nice warm room in Old Compton Street waiting. A nice class of customer. Proper gents some of them. A nice drop of brandy against the chill. It was nice and warm and comfortable. A nice little trade. She didn't need this rigmarole.

'A woman is such a contrary beast,' muttered Marsh.

8

It was April, with the worst of the weather behind them, when Swann planned his *Beauties* of *the British Empire*.

He'd met a Jamaican maid running errands in Bond Street and persuaded her to sit for a portrait. Her name was Sarah Cornwall and she belonged to a house in Park Lane. The owner of the house, a retired plantation man, had brought her back from the West Indies. She was a friendly woman, very black, with a belly the size of a kettledrum.

Kingdom Swann took her portrait and paid her three shillings. She looked pleased with the money but begged to go home. She was late and her master would be growing impatient. Swann tried to make her stay, asked her to look through the costume trunk, implored her to dress as the Queen of Sheba.

This idea made her hoot with laughter. She rocked back and forth and slapped her knees. The costume was only a copper crown and a pair of chiffon pantaloons. But her mood began to change when Swann explained that, should she decide to accept the crown, they would feel obliged to pay her two guineas.

'You just want to take me picture?' she said cautiously, unable to fathom the proposition.

'Yes,' he said.

She snorted. 'And when you've finished you'll change your tune and want to give me a knobbing!'

Cromwell Marsh gasped and dropped the lid of the costume trunk. Kingdom Swann looked aghast, staggered and grabbed his beard.

'I'm shocked!' said Marsh.

'I'm all struck down in a heap!' said Swann.

'I hope you wasn't supposing we wanted to make improper proposals,' said Cromwell Marsh sounding very upset.

'You just want to take me photograph?'

They nodded.

'And you want to give me two guineas?'

'Yes.'

Sarah Cornwall beamed. She was baffled. 'What's your game?' she said.

Then Marsh made his speech about beauty and art while Kingdom Swann approached her with flattery. She was very impressionable. At last, with the three shillings tucked safe inside a shoe, she promised to return on the second Sunday in the month and hurried from the shop.

'Did you ever see such a big, fine woman?' sighed Marsh, as they watched her from the window.

'She certainly knows how to fill a corset,' said Kingdom Swann.

'She's a marvel,' said Marsh, squashing his face against the glass as she disappeared from view.

'We'll do a new series of photographs,' said Swann. *'Beauties of the British Empire.* All we need are the costumes. We can start at the Gold Coast and work our way through to Zanzibar.'

'Wild women?' frowned Cromwell Marsh. 'Wild women in grass skirts and bracelets?'

'Yes.'

'Tropical women with the great big bums?'

'Yes.'

'I hope she don't forget,' said Marsh.

Swann spent several happy days painting a curtain with lavish banks of tropical flowers, exotic palms, butterflies, birds and a view of a distant volcano. He decorated the cloth with all the care and precision expected from a student of Fletcher-Whitby, gilding the feathers of every bird and not feeling satisfied until the palms were full of fruit and pollen glowed in the tongues of the flowers. The painting took him a week and when it was finished he felt tired but triumphant. His *Beauties of the British Empire* was going to be magnificent.

Sarah Cornwall kept her appointment. She arrived at the studio dressed in a hat and a Sunday frock. She was timid at first but they quickly made her comfortable. They found her a chair and let her play the phonograph. She watched Kingdom Swann load the camera while Cromwell Marsh brewed a pot of tea which she drank with gin to steady her nerves. Once the gin had taken effect she began to take off her clothes. She was stripped to her stays and ready for action when there was a terrible noise at the front of the shop.

'It's the police!' shouted Marsh. He ran across the room, hit the edge of the stage, fell forward and brought down the curtain and sneezed.

Swann was trying to imitate a pillar and Sarah was hiding under her hat when the intruder found them. He was a big bruiser with a heavy, weather-beaten face and a dab of yellow hair. He was wearing a threadbare suit and carried a hammer in his hand. He paused as he entered the studio, stared suspiciously around him, considered the camera, the costume trunk and the twitching curtain under the stage. He didn't know what to make of it. He scowled and weighed the hammer in his fist. And then he saw Sarah Cornwall.

'What have you done to my wife!' he bellowed.

'This lady is a famous artist's model,' blurted Marsh, emerging from his curtain. 'This lady has posed nude for royalty.' It was part of a speech he'd prepared for the police should he ever have the misfortune to meet them. He rehearsed it sometimes in his sleep.

'Model my arse! She's as daft as a brush. You think I don't know?' the husband thundered. He was breathing hard and his eyes were rolling. 'I followed her down from Park Lane. She came along here for a knobbing!'

He caught hold of Kingdom Swann and tapped the hammer against his nose. Swann's nose burst and his beard turned red. The husband, pleased with this display, drew back the hammer and hit him again.

'Shut your mouth and wait outside!' Sarah suddenly shouted. 'They're going to take me photograph!' She turned on her husband and stuck out her chest. She looked as mad as a turkeycock.

'You're half naked,' he protested.

'It's only pretend, I'm supposed to be historical. They're showing me off as royalty.'

'Oh, my Gawd!' shrieked the husband. He was horrified. He pushed Swann away and dropped the hammer. 'It's dirty pictures, is it?' His anger melted into grief. He was a broken man. He turned from the sight of his wife's disgrace, threw back his head and howled. He clutched at his face and fell to the ground. 'Oh, my Gawd! I hope Gawd strikes you blind, robbing a man of his own poor wife for the purposes of dirty pictures.'

'Robbing? We're paying her two guineas,' said Marsh.

'Two guineas?'

'That's more than a housemaid earns in a month,' said Marsh, a trifle indignantly.

'I'm not a housemaid, I'm a lady's maid,' said Sarah.

'Same difference,' said Marsh. 'Two guineas. And that works out about sixpence an inch, her being such a tall woman.'

'Sixpence!' seethed the husband. 'She's worth more than that, being a Negro and them so scarce. '

Sarah looked sullen, took up her chemise and stowed away her breasts. Kingdom Swann looked bilious.

'And don't forget the family grief,' continued the husband, beginning to warm to his theme. 'Think of the mischief it does to a man. How does he live with the shame of it? How does he manage to sleep at night, knowing that pictures of his wife without drawers is keeping company with thousands of strangers? How much do you pay *him*? That's what we have to consider here. How does he fit into the scheme?'

'We haven't taken any pictures,' said Swann, trying to plug his leaking nose. He collapsed into a chair and fumbled for a handkerchief. His drooping moustache was dripping blood.

'I'm not surprised!' roared the husband. 'A very dubious profession. A very dangerous business, purloining a wife on her way to church for the purposes of a dirty picture.'

'You'll find no mischief in it,' said Marsh. 'We keep a most scrupulous premises.'

'Mischief?' gasped the husband. 'I'd rather she was out for a knobbing than here for your dirty pictures. A knobbing is over before you know it and no harm done to the family but the shame of a dirty photograph can follow a husband into his grave. Mischief? It's a matter for the police, I shouldn't wonder.'

They were caught. There was nothing they could do but accept the terms he offered them. It cost them a full ten guineas before he agreed to take his wife home.

9

Cromwell Marsh was never trapped by the police, despite the vigilance of their agents. They raided photographic saloons from Hampstead to Holborn, destroyed pictures and imprisoned dealers but, in his opinion, such establishments invited trouble with their bold displays set out to catch the eye of the lewdster. Their windows were dressed with all manner of titillation so that none but the blind could fail to guess the true nature of their daily business.

There was nothing about the Swann premises to arouse suspicion. The window itself, tastefully furnished, contained a solitary Windsor & Newton easel bearing a print in an ebonised frame. Sometimes it was the scowl of a grocer that addressed the street and sometimes the scowl of a fishmonger's wife, always chosen from a small selection Marsh had saved for such purposes.

Nothing stronger than portraits of famous actresses might be purchased over the counter. A Kingdom Swann nude could only be obtained through the pages of the catalogue which was strictly limited to a list of grateful and wealthy subscribers. Discretion was everything. There were spies everywhere and the Indecent Advertisement Act of '89 had long since made it an offence to send doubtful material through the post.

Several times zealous members of the Society for the Suppression of Vice had entered the shop and endeavoured by fair means and foul to trick Cromwell Marsh into showing them something indecent.

They were middle-aged men with fat necks and confident manners. They generally began by expressing an interest in actresses and, having been presented with the entire stock of some five hundred portraits, and having found nothing there to outrage them, proceeded to make whispered enquiries into artists' models, female gymnasts or *poses plastiques*. At this point the zealous member would let it be known that he carried a large sum of money, should there be studies available.

'Artists' models, sir?' Marsh replied, cautiously, to one such enquiry from a small man in a green tweed suit and a military moustache.

'Artistic beauties in repose,' breathed the agent.

'They don't come more artistic than the stars of the London stage, sir,' Marsh assured him.

But the zealous member could not be persuaded. 'I'm in the mood for something a trifle exotic, if you grasp my meaning,' he whispered, pulling his ear and winking at Marsh.

Cromwell Marsh glanced furtively around him. He wiped the counter with the palms of his hands, as if he were planning to vault clean across it, run to the door and escape.

'Stimulating views of women expressing their loveliness,' continued the agent in a hoarse whisper. 'I'm looking for something slightly different. Something more exotic.'

Cromwell Marsh relaxed and smiled. 'I can see you're a connoisseur,' he murmured confidentially. 'A man of unusual refinement and taste.' He paused. Dramatically. And then he pulled forth a set of photographs of a very old woman dressed in feathers and buckskins. A blanket covered her shoulders and the buckskins trailed to the floor.

'What's this?' demanded the agent, screwing up his eyes as he puzzled over the portraits. He couldn't make any sense of them. He began turning them over in his hands.

'The epitome of pagan beauty,' declared Marsh. 'Passing Cloud, the last Red Indian Princess, late of Buffalo Bill's Wild West Show as seen by the Princess Mary of Wales in the sawdust ring at Earls Court. What d'you say to *that*, sir!' He stuck his thumbs in his waistcoat pockets and pushed out his chest triumphantly.

'I've plenty of money, if that's the problem,' growled the agent, throwing the photographs on to the counter. He was disappointed. He had thought he was going to make an arrest.

'I don't believe I've quite fathomed you, sir.'

'I've no time for this nonsense!' the agent hissed impatiently. 'I believe we're both men of the world and I've a stomach for something stronger!' And he leaned his weight against the counter, very agitated at the thought of confronting loathsome sights.

'I'm afraid you've lost me, sir,' said Marsh, doing his best to look hurt and perplexed.

The agent grew frustrated. The man must be an idiot! 'Women exposing themselves!' he growled. 'Young women exposing their *motherhoods!*' He made a fist with one hand and used it to saw the air into logs.

'Motherhoods!' gasped Marsh. He was trembling now and the blood had drained from his face. 'Do I believe my ears? Women exposing their motherhoods! I've never heard of such a disgrace and I'm a married man, sir, and blessed with children too. My wife was delivered of eight of them, three dead and five surviving and yet, I'm proud to say, as God is my witness, I've never seen over and above her knees!'

This was not so far from the truth since Cromwell Marsh had long since failed to be stirred by the sight of the frankly nude. When the fruit was peeled he found all the flavour lay with the peelings. For this reason he liked his wife to dress for bed like any other woman might dress for a night at the music hall. Warm wrappers delighted him, hot corsets excited him and the rustle of many petticoats drove the poor man to distraction. The more she wore the better he liked it.

'Don't play the innocent with me, dammit!' shouted the agent, very much embarrassed. 'I've never met a photographer yet who don't stoop to *some* depravity!'

'I think you've been given the wrong address,' returned Marsh, snorting and slapping the counter.

'It makes no difference – you're all the same!' raved the agent. 'Approaching fresh and attractive young women, seducing them with all manner of talk, luring them back to your filthy cellars, forcing them to smoke opium until they show you their motherhoods. The world is plagued with your kind of vermin.

It makes my skin crawl to think of what you do to 'em. Unless you're stopped there won't be a decent young woman in London who can feel secure beneath her skirt!'

'I don't like your attitude, sir!' thundered Marsh. 'I hope I shan't be obliged to run out and fetch the police!' And he threw such a fit of temper, such a fury of righteous indignation, that the zealous member fled to the street, fully convinced he had made a mistake.

No one outwitted Cromwell Marsh. His greatest adversary over the years proved to be Kingdom Swann himself, who refused to keep his light modestly under a bushel. The old man could find nothing indecent in their work and discussed it with anyone who would listen. It was, perhaps, this frank and open attitude, the obvious pride he took in his art, that persuaded others of his good intentions; although he was well protected, no doubt, by the power and influence of his many distinguished subscribers.

10

'Imust be nearly eighty years old,' grieved Swann. He sounded amazed, as if it had happened overnight. He held out his hands and stared at the shrivelled fingers.

'Fletcher-Whitby lived to be ninety,' said Cromwell Marsh, to comfort him.

'He was never attacked with a hammer,' sniffed Swann. His nose, which had split like a ripe fig, had taken a long time to knit. When the wound had finally healed, his nose had resumed its original shape but adopted different colours. It was yellow during the summer months with a touch of brass at the nostrils. Whenever the weather turned cold the nose turned a luminous shade of blue.

'There's some men your age would feel proud to be attacked by a jealous husband,' said Marsh, smoking a Turkish cigarette.

They were sitting in Hyde Park, watching the nursemaids on parade. It was a warm and peaceful afternoon with just enough of a summer breeze to rattle the canopy of trees. Domestics came strolling, arm in arm with soldiers, down to the Serpentine. A woman was walking a pair of poodles. Somewhere a brass band was playing.

'Jealous husbands?' said Swann. 'At my age it's ridiculous.' He sat on the bench in topcoat and gloves, with a newspaper spread on his knees like a rug.

'You're as fit as a flea,' said Marsh. 'I shouldn't wonder if you've strength left yet to father a child.'

'There's enough misery in the world,' grumbled Swann, poking the paper. 'Unemployment. Women on bicycles. Russians attacking British steamers. There's enough misery in the world without adding babies to the confusion.'

'A great artist like yourself has a duty to pass down his

genius,' said Marsh. A shame that Swann had been left without children.

'There's no guarantee that a son will follow his father,' said Swann, 'and besides, there's always the possibility of finding yourself with a daughter.'

'True,' sighed Marsh. 'That's very true and all the more reason, in my opinion, for having a larger family. The more of 'em you plant, so to speak, the greater the chance of finding you've passed on some small part of your genius.'

'Too late,' said Swann. 'The world has finished with genius.' He yawned and closed his eyes to signal the end of the argument.

Cromwell Marsh settled down to watch the nursemaids' parade. The breeze tugged their hats and pulled out the hems of their long, black skirts. Now and then the sun caught a shoe or glanced on a fatted calf. Marsh sat quietly counting them.

The peace was broken by shouts of alarm and the heavy honking of horns. Beyond the park a motorist had driven his machine into the wheels of an old haywagon. The horses bellowed and kicked in their traces, the wagon capsized in a storm of dust.

'Look at all that commotion!' growled Swann. 'They shouldn't let those machines on the road!'

'Motor cars is the future,' said Marsh as he strained to peer at the accident through the avenue of trees. He had been to the Motor Transport Show. He knew a thing or two about motors. At the Crystal Palace he'd seen family carriages lofty as galleons and narrow road-racers like armoured cigars. He'd seen stately Coventry Daimlers and rugged French Panhards. But Marsh had fallen in love with steam. Steam was speed. Fifty, sixty, seventy-five miles an hour. It was a Gardner-Serpollet steamer that had reached such a speed at the flying-start kilometre race in Nice. Seventy-five miles an hour! There was nothing to touch it.

'Dangerous,' said Swann. 'The wind alone is enough to knock out your eyes.'

Cromwell Marsh agreed. 'That's why they have to wear

those goggles,' he said, sucking on his cigarette. How it must feel to sit in the saddle, with the boiler boiling and the road running beneath your feet at seventy breathtaking miles an hour! Imagine!

'But what would happen,' said Kingdom Swann, 'in the likely event of a small collision?'

'How d'you mean?'

'Well, suppose, for the sake of argument, that you're whipping along at seventy miles an hour and you meet a flint or a cinder coming at you from the wrong direction. What happens?'

Cromwell Marsh shook his head.

'At such a speed that speck of stone would drill through human bone as neat as a hole in a button,' said Swann with considerable satisfaction. 'It would go through your face like a rifle bullet.'

Marsh chewed on his cigarette and stared thoughtfully through the trees. The wagon had been dragged to the side of the road. The traffic was moving again.

'I can't understand the fatal attraction,' said Swann, smoothing the newspaper over his knees.

'It's the speed of the road,' shrugged Marsh. 'The power of the machine.'

'Speed!' said Swann. 'Where's the advantage in all this speed?'

'It's obvious,' said Marsh, crushing the cigarette under his boot. But he didn't bother to explain.

'What's wrong with the horse? At least you can talk to a horse,' continued Swann. 'The next thing you know we'll have a mechanical army.'

'They already tried to organise some fancy corps of motor car volunteers,' said Marsh.

'They should have used 'em to chase the Boers.'

'That would have taught the buggers a lesson!' said Marsh and he chortled as he imagined it.

A small boy in a very dirty sailor suit came wandering out of the bushes. He wore a wooden sword in his belt and trailed a tin trumpet on a length of string. As he passed the two men he stopped to stare at Kingdom Swann's nose and give it a blast from the trumpet.

'I'm too old to be bothered by boys!' roared Swann. His eyes blazed and his beard began to bristle. He exploded through he newspaper and smacked the boy's head. The boy was so shocked that he fell on his sword and ran away screaming into the bushes.

'Did you see his face!' laughed Cromwell Marsh. 'The little bugger nearly pissed his pants! It's a shame you never had children.'

Swann sat back and stared at the sky. So much noise and commotion! He was tired. Dear God, he was almost dead. It was time to retire from the world.

But the world in the shape of Lord Hugo Prattle came knocking again at the door. When the Russian Baltic Squadron, hunting Japanese torpedo boats, settled instead for Great British trawlers, war fever swept the country. Newspapers printed daily accounts of the growing Russian threat. Novelty merchants sold paper lanterns, horsehair pigtails, mikado masks and strings of tiny, Japanese flags. Nothing could satisfy the public demand for news and views of brave Japan. Within a week of the Dogger Bank Outrage, Prattle had sent his request for studies of Japanese geisha girls. *Forbidden Views Through a Bamboo Curtain.* One dozen. All different.

Swann was reluctant but Prattle was stubborn and larded the old man with so much praise that he found it hard to refuse.

'It's all very comic,' he complained to Marsh, 'but where do we find this little woman? And what's to be done if she tells her husband? I thought we might have learned our lesson. You can't trust the work to amateurs.'

'She doesn't have to be a Japanese,' said Marsh. 'We can make her *look* like a Japanese. That's the art of it. That's what they do in the music halls. Think of the girls at the Coliseum.'

'The Coliseum?' said Swann, looking most perplexed. 'They've got Bonita and her Cuban Midgets at the Coliseum. But that doesn't mean they'll want to pose nude.'

'Midgets?' barked Marsh impatiently. 'We don't want no trouble with midgets. Forget the Coliseum. Think of Gilbert and Sullivan. *The Mikado*. Yum-Yum and NankiPoo.'

Swann smiled. He was beginning to understand. *'The Mikado!* That's more like it. Why, it must be twenty years ago. The Savoy. I took the late Mrs Swann.'

'Illusions,' said Marsh with a wave of his hand. 'Simple stage illusions. Find me some screens and a bowl of paper chrysanthemums – I'll build you a house in Yokohama. The geisha played by Ethel Spooner.'

'Ethel?'

'Gloria Spooner's sister Ethel.'

'She's built like a Suffolk punch!' hooted Swann. 'I'd like to see Gloria playing a geisha.'

'She's big,' said Marsh, 'and that's a fact. I can't deny that God built Gloria generous. But Ethel is small and as dainty as a sparrow. You'd never suppose they was sisters. The difference is remarkable.'

'I suppose we could paint her to look like a geisha,' said Swann rather doubtfully. Chalk on her face. Hair full of chopsticks. He pulled on his beard and considered the problem. 'I don't know,' he said, at last. 'The pictures we took would be counterfeits.'

'No more than your Biblical Beauties,' said Marsh sharply. 'Art is chiefly composed of conceits.'

So they sent for little Ethel Spooner and contrived to picture Prattle's dream. Ethel was bright and full of suggestions. She had worked with several photographers and felt comfortable with the camera. She'd been selling views of her bum since the time she was twelve years old. She didn't much care for Marsh but she liked the look of Kingdom Swann. He was large, untidy and affable, like a Wombwell Menagerie bear. She wasn't in the least alarmed by the colour of his nose.

They went to great pains to change her country of origin. They dressed her hair with combs and tassels, made a rosebud of her mouth and powdered her eyebrows white. They taught her to tie a kimono and flirt with a paper fan. It took them a week to catch the effect but the finished pictures were beautiful.

Prattle was delighted, of course, and gave his consent to publish the set for their catalogue. Marsh lost no time in printing them and to Swann's surprise they proved the most popular cards of the year. He retired the faithful Winchester and bought a Fallowfield's Saloon Universal in polished walnut on a patent ball-roller stand. He bought Marsh a new set of ivory teeth and Ethel a vulture-quill hat.

11

We beg to inform our friends, Marsh wrote in the catalogue, of *The Beauty of Japan*. Lately arrived from Yokohama, this lovely Lilliputian, already an accomplished geisha, is quite full-grown yet stands no taller that a child: the limbs very sweet and well-proportioned the breasts exquisite, the cherry blossom, which is most piquant, scarce broken from nature's bud. The subject, unwrapped from her silk kimono, is seen to be so small that she might be said to represent all womankind in miniature. She plays the flute, sings, composes poetry and was trained in the royal pavilions of pleasure.

Those who purchase this set may consider themselves the privileged and are promised to find delight in the sight of a geisha beauty so absorbed in her ritual toilet that she pays no heed to the camera and is nude in every particular. The views are thoughtfully arranged and will prove of enormous interest to the artist and armchair adventurer. They are guaranteed to stimulate the heart, please the eye and, in every way, afford uncommon satisfaction.

We are confident in our claims that these views are unique in London and cannot be repeated.

Available as a set of superior hand-coloured promenade prints.

One dozen. All different. £15.7s. 6d.

The Swann Studio. Piccadilly. London.

12

Kingdom Swann had found success. He was prized by collectors, loathed by other photographers and celebrated in all the best brothels in London. When Kingdom Swann exposed a girl's bum she became the very latest fashion, receiving gifts of champagne and pearls, invitations to intimate suppers and worthless proposals of marriage. Swann could transform gutter-snipes into fabulous objects of desire. And for this reason, London's more progressive madams went to great lengths to introduce him to the houri of their house. The old man did what he could to avoid them but his bad temper, his great age and his growing reluctance to work only helped to enhance his reputation.

Mrs Beeton, who owned the Villa Arcadia in Randolph Avenue, Maida Vale, persuaded him to picture her girls set out as a choir of dimpled angels. The girls, ten of the biggest in Christendom, rouged their nipples, powdered their curls and wore magnificent curving wings of goose feathers glued to canvas frames. They were angels fat enough for Rubens. They spread their legs and stretched their wings on a linen cloud stuffed with pillows and cushions.

The finished picture, printed on canvas and highly coloured, was mounted in a carved, gilt frame. It looked so like an Academy painting that many admirers were deceived and refused to believe that this work of art had been made by Swann's machine. Excited by the deception Swann spent several months making gum-print portraits, mixing colours with the emulsion and working the images with his brush. The results were foggy water-colours that pleased his eye but failed to win favour with regular patrons since the process destroyed so much definition.

The colour portraits on canvas, however, attracted a new class of customer. There were certain elderly gentlemen, recommended by Mrs Beeton, who wanted their mistresses photographed in scenes of artistic nudity. These reckless old bodgers, their brains curdled with lust, were mad enough to risk anything, even public scandal, for the chance to celebrate their lovers. Kingdom Swann's cleverly painted photographs were the perfect blend of lechery and romance, faithfully naturalistic yet exquisitely sentimental. And the pictures, sometimes printed so small they might have been pocket-book memorandums, at other times commissioned so large they'd have suited poster hoardings, proved surprisingly popular.

A steady procession of mistresses, from chamber-maids to delinquent daughters of obscure royal families, made secret visits to the studio. Some were seized with modesty and refused to remove so much as a glove and had to be soothed and showered with gifts from desperate benefactors before they were willing to flaunt their charms. Others, flattered to be taken for works of art, addressed the camera like ten shilling whores.

Swann treated them all to the same process of low art and high chemistry. The women were powdered until they shone and made to recline in a halo of light. Everything was done to enhance their beauty and that which God had failed to make perfect was neatly repaired in the darkroom. Scars were bleached out, breasts puffed up, creases and wrinkles dissolved in the wash. When the prints had been prepared Swann took his brush and tickled their fancies, coloured grey hair, restored missing teeth and made everything glow with a royal blush. And when all this had been done, with the subjects buried in glazes and paints, his patrons thanked him for such faithful copies of nature.

Mrs Beeton made a friend of the great photographer and sent her carriage, once a week, to collect him for afternoon tea. She was small of stature but as fat as a partridge. Her complexion was smooth and dark; the long hair thick and naturally curled; the eyes beautiful, black as tar; the nose prominent; the mouth very full and brightly painted. She wore a gown of gauze and lace and was wrapped, at all times, in a mist of Arabian perfume. She had, in her youth, been thought a beauty and posed as a slave-girl in Edwin Long's famous masterpiece, *The Babylonian Slave-Market*. In the comfort of her private suite, over many pints of hot, sweet tea, she told Kingdom Swann her story.

She had been born in Naples and decided at an early age to devote her life to the arts. She had studied in Paris and then, upon reaching England, attended Heatherley's, the most famous private art school in London where men and women mixed quite freely and both were encouraged to study the nude. She had been a clever and determined student. When she left she had hoped to establish herself as a water-colour artist. But they were difficult times. She sold her work but soon discovered she could not sell enough to pay the rent.

She was forced to earn a living by working as a model in other painters' studios. It was a disappointment but she enjoyed the company and the money wasn't bad. Her dark and romantic complexion attracted the attentions of Burne-Jones, Russell and Boothby, who gave her, at length, to Edwin Long. And it was there, as one of Long's winsome slave-girls, that she'd gained her first introduction to the wealthy dilettanti.

The painting, a vast canvas concerning the auction of a dozen young beauties-in-bondage, had been the sensation of the season. When it was shown at the Royal Academy the girls were already the toast of London. Politicians, architects and bankers fought for the pleasure of bedding them. Mrs Beeton regarded these engagements as theatrical performances and herself as a living work of art, an acrobatic automaton. Her energy and her enthusiasm did not go unrewarded.

The canvas was sold at Christie's in 1882 for more than six thousand guineas and she claimed she was then worth twice that amount from the proceeds of her marriage. While her face remained her fortune she'd accepted the hand of a wealthy poet with a weakness for spirits and spanking. Within six months she'd killed the old boar with kindness, inherited his money and a villa in Maida Vale.

Once again she was chased by wealthy admirers but now, in mourning, found it necessary to employ two girls to help entertain her callers. Men, she observed, no matter how lovesick, never refused her locums. Availability and enthusiasm were a woman's greatest virtues. As she employed more girls she treated them to all the disciplines of a well-trained theatre company. She claimed, and Swann never doubted it, that her girls were accomplished actresses. She was obviously very proud of them.

Mrs Beeton sipped at her tea and gazed about in satisfaction. The walls of her private rooms were lined with paintings and drawings. Above her head a luminous nude by Burne-Jones; at her elbow several life studies by William Boothby, executed in red chalks; beside the door pages from a Walter Crane sketchbook, lewd cartoons by Gilbert and Tenniel and, in place of honour, above the fire, a fine portrait of Mrs Beeton by the late, lamented, Edwin Long.

It was hard work, trying to manage a house of pleasure, but she found it rewarding. Her own desire to paint had been largely satisfied by decorating the villa. Each bedroom had been furnished according to the rules of some popular erotic dream. Among the most elaborate fancies were a seaside bathing machine, a Tuppenny Tube railway carriage and a famous funeral parlour. But her masterpiece was the Royal Victoria Suite. Here she had lavished both time and money to create a chamber fit for a queen. The walls were covered in tapestries, the floors were a showpiece of marquetry and everything, from the bed posts to the tablets of soap, had been embossed with the royal coat of arms. In these extravagant surroundings men would part with fortunes to get their hands on a set of imperial buttocks.

Her Majesty looked nothing at all like the portly parrot dressed in widows' weeds who had haunted the Isle of Wight. This was the Queen of an earlier age: the beautiful young woman who had taken the throne more than sixty years before and won the heart of Albert, son of the Duke of Saxe-Coburg-Gotha. Mrs Beeton had found her working at the tea rooms in Drury Lane.

54

The likeness was uncanny and she was the darling of all the Indian maharajahs who took a special delight in forcing their hands up her skirts.

'It seems to drive 'em wild, Mr Swann,' said Mrs Beeton happily. 'There's not one of them I've met can resist the idea of shafting the British Empire.'

'It's a sobering thought,' said Swann.

'They mean her no harm,' she assured him. 'Indeed, they treat her like royalty. I've never known a girl to be showered with so many gifts and favours. Since she came to the throne she's been presented with ivory, jade and any number of tiger skins.'

'Remarkable!'

'She's a most remarkable invention,' said Mrs Beeton with more than a touch of pride. 'But they're never satisfied, Mr Swann. Oh, but they're greedy devils! I could have sold her a dozen times, without exaggeration. And when they're not wanting to buy her from me they're trying to steal her slippers or pocket a tablet of soap.'

'They steal the soap?' said Swann. 'I should have thought they were born of a better class than the sort that pilfers soap.'

'It's by way of a souvenir. Since I take the trouble to have the soap embossed with the royal crest I conclude they take it home as a keepsake.'

Swann reflected on the weakness of the maharajahs while Mrs Beeton cut him a slice of almond cake. 'If you'd allow me the pleasure of taking her photograph,' he suggested, at last, 'she might offer each guest a carte-de-visite and you'd save yourself some expense.'

'It's an inspiration, Mr Swann! If it puts you to no trouble I'll send her over in my carriage at your earliest convenience.'

13

Three days later, at an early hour, Queen Victoria stepped down from the carriage in Piccadilly. She was wrapped in a coat and carried her crown in a hat box.

Although the old man had warned Cromwell Marsh of her startling physiognomy, when the woman walked into the studio the sight fully chilled his marrow. Beneath her coat she was dressed in coronation robes and a wealth of ribbons and medals. When she asked to see the photographer he grinned and grovelled and wrung his hands and had to be rescued by Swann, who whisked the Queen away and saw she was sitting comfortably, out of harm's reach, on the stage.

'It's bleeding cold,' she puffed, pulling open the hat box and screwing the crown to her head. 'I hope I don't have to pose with my tits and bum hanging out.'

'Make up the stove!' ordered Swann, as Marsh came creeping into view. 'Her Majesty feels there's a chill in the air that threatens to do her some mischief.'

'And find us something hot to drink!' the Queen shouted cordially. 'Good and strong and plenty of sugar.'

Marsh tried to speak but choked on his words. He could only stand and stare at the Queen, bobbing his head forlornly. He was so flustered by the event, so intimidated by her perfumed corpulence, that he half-believed they'd been given a royal appointment.

'Blimey, what's wrong with him?' asked the Queen in surprise, when he'd gone to fill the kettle.

Kingdom Swann tapped his skull and sighed. 'He's wrong in the head,' he whispered.

'Why don't they have him locked away?' breathed the Queen, excited by this faint whiff of danger.

'Oh, he's harmless enough,' said Swann. 'But you couldn't describe him as being quick-witted. I'm training him to sweep the floors and fetch and carry for me although, when he gets himself excited, he tends to fall down or wet his drawers.'

'Is he going to get excited?' she enquired rather cautiously, pressing a hand to her throat and puffing out a generous chin. 'I hope I don't encourage him.'

Swann smiled and shook his head. 'He's no understanding of the fully fashioned female form,' he confided. 'It's all the same to him. He may have the body of a man but his brains have never properly grown and he thinks like a ten-year-old girl.'

'Poor sod!' said the Queen, watching Marsh creeping back with the kettle, walking on tiptoe and bobbing his head.

'Yes,' said Swann. 'It's sad to watch him struggling. But he's perfectly good-natured and always willing to work.'

'I don't like the way he keeps looking at me,' the Queen confessed beneath her breath as she caught Marsh grinning and winking his eye while he waggled the poker in the stove.

'We could lock him away in the darkroom,' suggested Swann.

'No. I've had to entertain worse than him,' she said, shrugging off her fears. 'Men can be bleeding queer when they see you dressed as royalty.'

'It can't be easy,' said Kingdom Swann, 'to be born as the ghost of the Queen.'

'You never know how it's going to take them,' she sighed. 'There's some as fall down on their hands and knees and want to do nothing but suck on your toes. And there's some treat you worse than nobody, pulling and poking your parts like a freak in a travelling show.'

When the stove was blazing and they'd quaffed several pints of scalding tea, Swann settled down to work. He planned to photograph the Queen, with considerable pomp and circumstance, beside a papier mâché throne.

She pulled off her shoes and rummaged under her petticoats to unlace a pair of satin drawers. They were a voluminous article, trimmed in gold with scalloped lace and embroidered with the royal crest. When the drawers had drifted down to her feet she kicked them carelessly over the stage and into the trembling, outstretched hands of a half-demented Cromwell Marsh.

'He's pinched my drawers!' shouted the Queen as she watched him struggle to stuff this warm and fragrant treasure into his jacket pocket.

Marsh looked alarmed and began to shuffle away, colliding with the camera stand and overturning a chair.

'Come back here!' shouted Swann.

Marsh shook his head. His jaw was working and his hair was standing in ginger spikes. He looked bewildered, like a man waking up from a dream.

'Stop!' roared Swann.

Marsh gave out a strangled cry, wrapped his arms around himself and sprinted for the studio door.

'Oh, let the silly sod have his fun!' laughed the Queen. 'I'm always losing my drawers.'

'It's dreadful!' cried Swann, running in circles. 'What shall I say to Mrs Beeton?'

'Don't mention it,' said the Queen, stepping lightly down from the stage. 'I lose a dozen pairs of drawers a week.'

'What happens to them!'

The Queen shrugged. 'They're generally stolen as souvenirs. Sometimes they wear them. Sometimes they sport them as handkerchiefs. There's one old boy who likes me to knot them around his head and whip his bum with a swagger stick. He bends over the bed with his bum sticking up in the air and makes me beat him black and blue.'

'Good God!' gasped Swann.

'He's always most apologetic,' said Queen Victoria sweetly. 'He blames the Indian army.'

Swann hurried after Marsh but lost him in the street. He watched him running through the bustling crowd like a common pickpocket chased by the police. The poor photographer stood, astonished, until he had disappeared from view.

'Did you catch him?' asked the Queen as she wandered into the front of the shop.

Swann shook his head. 'His brains have gone wrong,' he muttered and this time he said it with greater conviction.

'He looked so wild for a moment I thought he was going to make a spectacle of himself,' said the Queen and shivered at the prospect.

Swann pulled down the blind at the window, locked the door and asked the Queen to return to her throne. She needed very little encouragement. She hitched her coronation robes to her waist in order to show off the shape of her legs and the cut of the royal whiskers. In one hand she carried a sceptre, in the other she weighed an imperial breast.

These photographs of Victoria were among the most highly prized pieces of work to emerge from the Kingdom Swann studio. They were never sold from the catalogue and those lucky enough to receive a print were never inclined to part with them. They proved so scarce that even Lord Hugo Prattle failed to obtain one for his library. The prints were numbered and given away, as souvenirs, to the most distinguished foreign guests to stay at the Villa Arcadia. They were coloured by Swann and mounted in tiny cardboard frames which were signed by Mrs Beeton in a flourish of purple ink.

Vivat Regina Vaginarum.

14

And what of Violet Askey? How did she fill her days?
She was not, as Swann supposed, content to guard the
groceries in the house near Golden Square. She was not,
as Marsh recommended, employed in the search for a suitable
husband. Encouraged by her modernist friends she attended
meetings of the Women's Freedom Movement. She heard Mrs
Fawcett speak on the Revolutionary Suffragettes and Mrs
Pankhurst, whom she thought rather plain, declare it was time
to shake men awake with the sound of broken window panes.
She began to understand that, until women were granted their
proper place in society, there could be no peace in the world.
Women must be granted their independence to influence the
nation's affairs. They must be sent to parliament where they
could implement their great reforms. And, if men refused to
relinquish power, then women must take to the streets and fight.

She became a militant supporter of the Ladies Vegetarian
League. Men were brutes because they lived like brutes, hunting and killing and feeding on flesh. The belly fed the brain and
a man might be tamed, like any wild beast, with a diet of white
fish, milk and honey.

Kingdom Swann pined for a hot beef pie but dared not
complain about his suppers. It was a small price to pay to have
his housekeeper in such fine spirits. Her temper improved and
she seemed, at times, to be quite jolly. When she asked for an
increased allowance he doubled the amount requested. He
would never have guessed that it found its way into the coffers
of the suffragettes. It amused her to know that the profits he
made from the plight of women should be used towards their
emancipation. And poor Swann, working hard for women's
rights, didn't have the least suspicion.

He was preparing a new set of postcards. The wrestling craze had come to town. In an exhibition at Olympia, Madrali the Terrible Turk did battle with the famous George Hackenschmidt. Lord Hugo Prattle, always hungry for novelty, ordered two dozen wrestling scenes. He sent his request with a copious list of instructions. The studio to provide a pair of fighting fortresses, each no more than twenty years old and skilled in the ways of the noble art. The first to be fierce and very large with broad flanks and a fair complexion. The second to be a fitting opponent, the eyes and hair dark in the Spanish manner, the limbs inclined to be fat and delicious. The wrestlers once in the heat of battle should be turned at frequent intervals so that neither girl could be said to have the advantage. Long hair preferred. Large feet essential. The cards to be cut and coloured by hand.

They found gladiators in Gloria Spooner and a laundry-girl called Gladys Pickles. Gladys wanted to be a singer and dancer. She was a good-looking girl who had once been mistaken for Nellie Melba. Gloria had told her that lots of famous dancers had been discovered through private pictures. They took the stage with their hair in braids and their bodies gleaming with coconut oil. But the secret of wrestling eluded them.

'I'm too old for acrobatics,' puffed Gloria as they helped her into a head twist and strangle. 'Why can't you do me as Jezebel?'

'Yes,' piped Gladys. 'It might be helpful if we understood the story.' She was under the impression they had come to perform an erotic ballet.

'Story?' said Marsh, in a very superior tone of voice. 'These days art don't have stories!'

'Think of yourselves as Amazons,' said Kingdom Swann gently, 'locked together in mortal combat.'

'I was a Beauty from Bible Land,' grumbled Gloria as Gladys practised her hammerlock.

It was a busy time for Swann, shut away in the studio, watching the girls rehearse their battle. He should have been watching Violet Askey. She ran riot in Smithfield Market, throwing stones at butchers' boys.

15

'I heard there were twenty thousand of them. And all shouting like socialists,' said Lord Hugo Prattle, grinding his teeth with excitement.

'More like two hundred thousand,' said Swann. 'I've never seen such a multitude.'

'Were they angry?' said Prattle. 'Did they fight? What did they want, I've never seen one.' He stopped walking and wiped at his whiskery face with a lace-embroidered handkerchief.

'They look regular enough,' said Swann. 'Shop-girls, house-maids, mothers and daughters. It's every size and shape of woman and all of them calling for the vote. They say they're going to change the world.'

'You can't change the world with scraps of paper,' snorted Prattle, looking perplexed. 'You need cavalry. No work for women.'

It was late June 1908. Kingdom Swann had been invited to stay at Prattle House in Dorset to conduct a series of photographs. The house had originally been a priory, purchased during the Reformation as a breeding ground for the Prattle family. After fire and flood in the eighteenth century the house had been rebuilt with the help of too many architects. The architects had squabbled and the work had not been completed. Within its bulging walls there were rooms without doors and staircases running nowhere. It was a maze of back alleys and sunless corridors. Approached from the ornamental drive the house looked more like a factory disguised with a pagan temple facade and crowned by curious turrets and towers. But the ancient gardens and lakes survived. Lord Hugo Prattle, in pensive mood, was walking the old photographer through the gardens and asking for news of the suffragettes. Swann had been at the Hyde Park rally and was trying, in vain, to describe the event.

'It was worse than the Coronation. They filled Hyde Park and all the surrounding streets. They stopped the traffic for miles around. Hundreds of thousands of them. There were marching bands and flags flying the green, white and purple. A great, foaming ocean of petticoats.'

'So many women in the world,' sighed Prattle, pausing to snap a rose. 'So many women and so little time. *Vita brevis*. It breaks a man's heart.'

He twirled the rose between finger and thumb, wafting the perfume under his nose. 'I don't suppose you have any studies?' he said hopefully. *'The Suffragette Surrenders? Suffragette in a Silk Wrapper?* I don't yet have a suffragette.' He might have been an entomologist, discussing a rare and exotic beetle.

Kingdom Swann shook his head.

' "Alas! The love of women! It is known to be a lovely and a fearful thing," ' grieved Prattle, throwing down the flower. 'Who said that?'

'Byron,' said Swann.

'Was it, by thunder!' said Prattle. He seemed surprised.

There was a splash from the far shore of the lake that shook the crows from the trees. Prattle trampled to a hole in the hedge and pulled a telescope from his coat.

'What is it?' said Swann, peering anxiously over his shoulder.

'The housekeeper,' said Prattle, twisting the telescope against his eye. 'The housekeeper's in the lake again!'

'Has there been an accident? Is the woman in trouble?'

'Miss Petersen in trouble?' laughed Prattle. 'Couldn't sink Miss Petersen. Learned to swim with the porpoises.'

'But how did she come to fall in the lake?' cried Swann.

'She didn't fall,' said Prattle. 'Jumped. Always jumping into the lake. She came across on the boat from Norway.'

'What?' shouted Swann in confusion. 'What?'

'She's a Norwegian. They're devils for theories of organic vigour. The sort of women who eat fruit for breakfast and like to suffer cold-water plunges. Whenever she thinks I'm out of the way she slips down here for the exercise.'

'Swimming in the lake?'

'Well, sir, I'll admit it's a queer sort of habit,' grinned Prattle. 'But she's a damn pretty sight, for all that, and she leads the other girls a dance. One night, last summer, caught her down here with the kitchen-maids, splashing around like fishes.'

He turned away and rubbed his face, his eyes dazzled by the sunlit water. She was too far away to be admired with any degree of satisfaction. 'No more time to waste in the garden,' he said briskly. 'Take you into the library – show you my collection.' He turned and marched through the shrubbery, hacking out a path for himself with strokes from the big, brass telescope.

The library was a long hall with a marble floor, the walls lined with shelves and glass cabinets. Heavy damask curtains had been drawn at the windows to guard against the light. Swann stepped forward slowly, blinking into the gloom. Here was Lord Prattle's notorious hoard of erotic books and manuscripts, prints, paintings and photographs.

Among the groaning shelves were portfolios of work by James Gillray and Thomas Rowlandson, a sketchbook of dreams by James Henry Fuseli, priceless Japanese pillow-books and a set of rare engravings by the Belgian master, Felicien Rops. These treasures rubbed shoulders with badly printed confessions and poor translations of lewd French novels, and all the shelves had a fine bloom of dust, since his lordship thought of nothing but camera studies.

An oak gallery ran around the library and, upon this second level, the bookshelves continued, fading into the cobwebs that clouded the vaulted ceiling. At the far end of the hall stood a black marble fireplace, its chimney-piece stuffed with fetish objects and its hearth girdled by large armchairs. A table, crowded into a corner, supported a heavy Hindu bronze of a monkey and woman locked in love. Beside it an oak lectern, carved in the shape of a grinning, ithyphallic satyr, held open a volume of photographs. Prattle had contrived to gather photographs of every class and colour of woman, laid bare,

Acrobat to Zulu, in one hundred leather volumes. It had taken nearly twenty years and there was always some new work to be done. Women frustrated him by getting everywhere. There was no end to his labour.

His lordship guided Swann around the museum, pausing here and there to discuss an exhibit. In ten of the big glass cabinets were souvenirs and tokens from a thousand brief encounters with women. There were button shoes and silk slippers, stockings, hat-pins, locks of hair and various scraps of underwear. Every item in the remarkable display bore a neat paper label inscribed with a number according to some obscure classification of Prattle's own invention.

He was very proud of the museum. It was a rare life's work. He had never married although he thought there might be children scattered somewhere in the world. He was the last of the Dorset Prattles. He didn't know what would happen to the house, or the collection, when he died. He supposed the bastards would fight for them.

The thought threw him into a melancholy. Swann had been brought from London for a special series of photographs to be used as studies for a monument, a memorial in stone. When Prattle passed from the world he wanted to be sure that something of his work survived. They might demolish the house but they wouldn't rob his tomb. He planned to be buried, with his one hundred leather albums, beneath a massive weight of stone. Kingdom Swann would take pictures as a guide for the sculptor. Nothing elaborate. A study of Prattle, dead in bed, surrounded by seven of the upstairs maids.

'Large as life and twice as natural,' he said, sketching on the air with his hands. 'Gone to sleep for eternity in a circle of snow-white bums.'

It made Kingdom Swann feel uneasy. 'I don't like to hear you talk of such things,' he said. 'It's a long time before you'll have to make arrangements.'

'Drop dead tomorrow,' said Prattle, puffing out his cheeks. 'Who knows? Marked the grave beside the lake. Fine view of the house.'

'You'll live to be a hundred,' said Swann.

Prattle considered the possibility, closed one eye and pulled on his moustache. 'Nineteen hundred and fifty four,' he said at last. 'We might all be living under the sea like Captain Nemo or taking flights around the moon. The world will have changed almost beyond our recognition. They'll look back at what we've achieved and laugh. There'll be no crime, no poverty and they'll probably have found an inoculation to cure every known disease. The French will have ceased to exist, that's certain. There will be an inoculation for 'em. We'll grow into a race of giants where the women are always willing, softly spoken and ten feet tall.'

'And a man will grow two heads in order to conduct a conversation with himself,' said Swann.

Prattle eyed him suspiciously. 'They'll be exciting times,' he declared, locking the museum.

'I'll not live to see it,' said Swann. He sniffed. 'Don't care for it. You can keep tomorrow and good riddance. Live in the past. That's my advice. You know where you are with yesterday.'

Prattle didn't like to argue with him. He retired to the master bedroom and practised the look of the dead.

'A man looks his best when he's dead,' he declared. 'Saw plenty of it during the war. Old men looking as sweet as babies. No reason. One of God's little jokes.'

Swann set up his equipment and when he was ready Prattle rang a bell. The maids, coarse and well-fed country girls, shuffled naked into the room and settled themselves on the floor. None of them seemed in the least surprised by their master's odd request. They'd been washed and powdered for the event and their heads neatly wrapped in black silk veils. They knelt beside the funeral bed and did their best to look bereaved.

They were chaperoned by Miss Petersen, the amphibious housekeeper, wearing a modest afternoon dress and a lace cap pinned to a bundle of fine, blonde hair. She was a tall, athletic woman who quietly sat in a chair beside Swann to monitor the proceedings. She saw the event as a frank display of English physical culture. It was rather a morbid presentation but you couldn't expect too much from these curious, red-faced foreigers.

'Mr Swann is an artist,' said Prattle, by way of introduction. 'A great man. A photographer. He's going to turn you into angels. Follow his instructions.'

'Thank you,' said Swann and settled down to work.

But Prattle could not rest in peace. How were the maids arranged? He couldn't see them from his pillow. Should they swoon in a circle with their arms outstretched or throw back their heads to heaven? Several times Kingdom Swann was made to occupy the bed while the corpse climbed out to view the effect.

As the afternoon deepened the maids became bored, began to yawn and whisper and fidget. It was suffocating in the veils and the threadbare carpet hurt their knees. Prattle tried to revive their interest. He spoke to them like a general addressing his troops before battle. Think of the glory. Eternal youth. Solid marble. Tits like tusks. Every bum a work of art. Something to make your mothers proud. And he promised them each an extra five shillings. *Vita brevis, ars longa.*

16

It was during his time at Prattle House that Swann met Stanley Gaunt, the pioneer balloonist. Gaunt had been on the maiden flight of his new dirigible, *Ostrich,* when a summer storm had driven him down on Lord Hugo Prattle's estate. He'd arrived at the door at midnight, exhausted, bleeding and covered in mud. They could see no sign of his ship through the rain and assumed that he'd fallen overboard and tumbled out of the sky.

But the next day Swann woke up to find the *Ostrich* floating in the trees beyond the ornamental lake. He leaned from the bedroom window and squinted into the sunlight, unable to believe his eyes. It was an inflated canvas sausage, some thirty feet in length, with a metal contraption strapped to its belly. The sky was fresh and clean. The airship pulled at its anchor as the big, blunt nose nudged the morning breeze.

At breakfast he could barely contain his excitement as Prattle introduced him to the brave young aviator. Stanley Gaunt, heir to Gaunt's beef gravy empire, was sitting at table eating a kipper. He looked as pretty as a young Greek god. His eyes were bright and very blue and his teeth were as dainty as pearls. He was dressed in riding breeches and a leather coat. The top of his head was wrapped in a bandage. He greeted Swann warmly and apologised for his rather untidy appearance. He had been sailing from Glastonbury to Dorchester when a freak gust of wind had driven the ship from her course and damaged part of the rigging.

'Knocked me clean from the saddle!' he laughed, tapping his bandaged head. 'It was lucky I didn't drown in the lake.'

After breakfast he took them down to admire the ship.

'She's beautiful!' cried Swann as they approached the

Ostrich through the trees. The balloon creaked and pulled at her moorings. The rigging supported a bicycle frame mounted above a petrol engine. The engine drove a wooden propeller. The pilot, sitting on the bicycle saddle, could steer the craft by manipulating a primitive rudder.

Stanley Gaunt grinned. 'She's beautiful,' he agreed. 'But she's also inclined to be temperamental.'

Prattle was less than impressed. He surveyed the ship and shook his head. 'She's just a big bag of wind!'

'I've seen some changes in my time,' said Swann, shielding his eyes against the sun. 'I was born before the public railways. Can you believe it? Yes. It's true. I've seen some changes but I never thought I would live to see men fly.' He turned and grasped the aviator's hand.

'Oh, this is nothing! One day there will be airships serving the empire,' laughed Stanley Gaunt. 'Airships the size of Cunarders, seating a thousand people in comfort.'

'I won't see it,' said Swann.

'It's not far away,' said the aviator. He planned to hang a cabin from the rigging with room enough for his first passenger. The cabin had been ordered from a Coventry coach builder and would bear the legend:

COOKS LOOK UP TO GAUNT'S BEEF GRAVY.

'None of us will live to see it!' snapped Prattle in a cantankerous mood. 'The Americans are building aeroplanes.' He turned to the aged photographer. 'What's their name? The White brothers.'

'Wright,' said Gaunt.

'Yes,' said Prattle. 'The White boys are having a lot of success with their heavier-than-air machines. That's the shape of the future. Machinery in the shape of birds. They'll soon build 'em big as locomotives. And there's an end to your gas sausage.'

'There's no future in aeroplanes,' smiled Gaunt. 'I'll admit they look very dashing. But give 'em a nudge in the wrong direction, the tail twists and they start to spin. They're a menace in the sky.'

'They're flying,' said Prattle stubbornly. 'Despite what you say, sir, they're flying.'

'A fluke,' said Gaunt. 'No more than a lucky accident that turns the natural laws upside down.'

'Isn't that enough?' said Prattle.

Gaunt shook his head. 'It can't last forever,' he said. 'They're too heavy to hang in the clouds. I went to the London Aero Club Trials last year. Everything they threw in the air fell down again.'

'Accidents?' whispered Swann, fearfully.

'A regular firework display,' said Gaunt.

Kingdom Swann was shocked. He felt convinced that airships, alone, were destined to conquer the skies. He looked up and saw a miracle. A slow and buoyant leviathan. And it seemed to him, standing that morning in the long, wet grass beneath the tethered canvas cloud, there could be nothing more beautiful in the whole of the world than the sight of this silent airship.

'There's no speed in these old gas bags,' said Prattle.

'Speed!' snorted Swann. 'Where's the advantage in all this speed?'

'Speed is power,' said Prattle. 'One day they'll build aeroplanes with *twenty* engines, big enough to fly to the moon.'

'But where's the advantage?' insisted Swann.

'Advantage, sir?' shouted Prattle. 'It's obvious!' And he lumbered away to spit in the lake. He wished that the stranded airman had been a fat, young woman. It was such an opportunity. It was such a waste. A fat, young woman who wasn't afraid to sport her mutton. He peered into the rigging, dreaming of buttocks to fit the saddle. Goggles and gloves. *Ascent of the Aviatrix. Companion to Artist, Actress and Acrobat.*

'An airship is designed to float. That's the secret of their success, ' Stanley Gaunt told Swann. 'So there's no limit to the size of them.'

'I heard the new Zeppelin carried fifteen passengers,' said Kingdom Swann.

'Why, that's just the beginning,' said Gaunt. 'One day we'll be living in floating cities moored high above the earth!'

'How does it feel to have your head in the clouds?' grinned Swann. 'Can you breathe them? Are they poisonous?'

The aviator stroked his chin and stared thoughtfully into the sky. 'It's like riding the waves in a fabulous sea,' he said at last. He smiled. His face shone beneath the turban.

'What can you see from such a height? I can't imagine it,' said Swann.

'It can't be described, sir. The words have yet to be invented. When you're flying high above a village you look down to earth and it's like staring over an angel's shoulder. There, beneath you, cluster the cottages, the meadows and hedgerows, ponds and ditches. And you know that people have probably lived in those little dwellings and laboured in those fields for more than a thousand years. But *you* are the first man in history, the first man in the whole world, to have seen such things from the sky.' He paused and tossed his lovely head, gazing heroically into the sun. 'I don't know. There's nothing like it on earth. Everything looks so different. Perhaps the soul might catch a glimpse of it, rising from the body at death. It must be the view that God commands of the world. You're a photographer. You should be up there taking pictures.'

'The man's an artist!' shouted Prattle from the water's edge. 'He's not interested in views!'

'I think he'll change his mind,' said Gaunt. 'When the *Ostrich* has finished her trials I'll take him aloft and show him the world.'

Swann needed no encouragement and, despite his lordship's strong disapproval, promptly accepted the invitation.

When the *Ostrich* was fitted with the cabin he would be first to take a ride. Gaunt thought she might be ready at the end of September and promised to keep Swann informed of her progress. Swann took several photographs of the ship and returned to London in high spirits.

17

He tried to imagine dirigibles ploughing the city fogs, ferrying people, parcels and livestock, fleets of them anchored over the Thames. One day every man might have a balloon, moored on a pole in his own backyard. Perfect for parties and summer picnics. Eventually they would build the first transatlantic airships, twice the size of the *Mauretania*, complete with restaurants and aerial ballrooms.

It was the birth of a new age. The old maps were worthless. You could scratch a national frontier in rock but you couldn't chalk a line in the sky. How would future wars be fought, now that armies could sail over mountains? Such an army would be invincible! An armada of floating battleships, seen from the ground like specks on the wind, a scatter of deadly seeds. How could you stop them? Perhaps they would try to divide the sky with lines of tethered balloons, marking out the frontiers, British clouds, French clouds, a preposterous national washing line. But if every army took to the air no one would dare to mount an invasion. War would become impossible. Or perhaps the battle would be for the sky? Big airships, armed with cannon, colliding like Spanish men o' war. The clouds red with blood. The dead and the wounded raining to earth. Absurd! Airships weren't built for battle. They were fat and gentle traders. Treasure ships for the empire. Galleons to a golden age.

The newspapers that summer were full of the Wright brothers' tour of Europe. Swann waited impatiently for word from Stanley Gaunt. On the 25th July he received a letter from the aviator. The *Ostrich*, fitted with her new cabin, would be ready for flight in September. The photographer was invited aboard on the 20th of the month for a voyage from Portsmouth to the Isle of Wight. Sandwiches and champagne would be served.

'You need your head examined!' said Marsh, when he heard the news. 'You're far too old to risk life and limb in some half-witted aerial stunt. A man your age should have some respect for his self.'

'You're never too old for adventure,' said Swann. 'I'm surprised *you* haven't tried flying machines – you're a devil for the motor car…'

'That's different,' said Marsh. 'I like to keep my feet on the ground. That's the way God planted 'em.'

Swann grinned and peered at the stage through the camera. They were working on *The Dreams of Hercules* or *Classical Temptations*. Hercules, wearing nothing but helmet and sandals, was sprawled asleep in a bed of straw while a naked succubus knelt over him. The part of the succubus was played by Gladys Pickles. Hercules was played, without conviction, by a coalman called Lanky Parsons.

He was a lugubrious individual with pointed ears and a penis the size of an exhibition salami. No one could remember exactly how Lanky had first been persuaded to wave his penis in public. It wasn't something he liked to talk about. He found its tremendous dimensions neither practical nor ornamental, it was a burden to carry, a devil to conceal and his wife would have nothing to do with him. She always maintained that had she but known his secret before the wedding night she would never have entered the marriage. He felt very bitter towards his Creator. He was still a virgin and making a spectacle of himself was his only satisfaction.

'Ain't frigging nature cruel enough without men dreaming of growing wings?' he demanded from his bed of straw.

'Go back to sleep,' ordered Swann. 'You're supposed to be dreaming of Gladys.'

Lanky grunted and let the helmet fall over his face. 'You can't expect men to stir up the clouds without something nasty happening,' he muttered. 'They're going to do some damage with all their frigging contraptions. The sky is a very delicate skin – it's like a big blister around the earth – and once it gets punctured all the oxygen will escape. They're flying their machines too high. That's what's happening. One day we'll hear a deafening fart and then we'll die of suffocation. The weather has changed since they started flying. You can't deny it. I've never known such weather. You can't fiddle with nature. If you fiddle with nature you breed frigging monsters.'

'Look at you,' said Cromwell Marsh, by way of illustration.

'Look at me,' said Lanky Parsons, pulling on his salami.

'Well, I think it's wonderful!' piped Gladys, suddenly jumping to her feet. Gladys, in contrast to Lanky, had grown rather proud of her attributes and considered herself to be the outstanding nude of her generation. She walked up and down the stage, sticking out her chest and striking provocative poses. 'I think Mr Swann is such a brave man!'

'You've got a brain like a frigging cauliflower!' shouted Lanky Parsons impatiently.

'And you're a very ill-tempered man,' returned Gladys, cupping her hands to her breasts. 'You're coarse and cheap and I'll thank you not to point your anatomy at me.'

'It's not my fault,' said Lanky. 'That's the way it grows.'

'Let's get back to work,' said Swann, clapping his hands. 'If we don't catch it soon we'll lose the light.'

'Tell him to stop waving his anatomy, Mr Swann,' demanded Gladys. 'He's making me feel queasy.'

'It's the frigging straw,' grumbled Lanky. 'It's scratching me something wicked. I just can't seem to get comfortable.'

'Now I've lost the mood, I'm so upset,' said Gladys, stamping her foot and threatening to leave the stage.

'Would you like me to fetch you a glass of water?' said Swann.

Gladys shook her head. 'I'd like a cup of tea,' she said, hopefully, 'and perhaps a small slice of cake.'

'No time!' shouted Cromwell Marsh, anxiously watching the shadows as they spread across the studio floor. 'We're wasting the light. Go and torment Hercules.'

'I can't bear to look at him,' said Gladys, but she clambered back into the straw.

'Perhaps he's right,' said Marsh, as the company settled

down again and the first of the plates had been exposed. 'You can't expect men to float in thin air.'

'Nonsense!' grinned Swann. 'One day we'll all be cresting the clouds.'

18

On the 18th September, two days before Swann's flight, Stanley Gaunt took the *Ostrich* from her moorings at Glastonbury and set sail for Portsmouth. A brass band was playing and a crowd of several hundred spectators assembled to see the airship launched. Gaunt made a speech about aviation for the benefit of the *Glastonbury Weekly Observer*. A barrel of beer was tapped for the benefit of the crowd. At one o'clock, sharp, pocket watches were consulted, a pistol was fired and the *Ostrich* took to the sky.

The weather was fine with a brisk wind. Visibility was perfect and for a few glorious hours cooks looked up to Gaunt's beef gravy. But the *Ostrich* never reached her destination. Twelve miles from Ringwood she abruptly lost height and ran against a church spire. The balloon exploded. The cabin collapsed. Stanley Gaunt fell to earth in flames.

'The bugger fell down!' hooted Cromwell Marsh, when he read the account in the morning paper. 'I told you it was too good to be true. The bugger fell out of the sky!'

The shock of the disaster nearly put an end to Kingdom Swann. He had missed an appointment with death by a whisker. His suitcase was packed and his flying clothes waiting. He'd purchased a portable camera especially for the flight. An airship was designed to float. That was the secret of their success. He had seen it with his own eyes. You couldn't sink a dirigible. He couldn't believe Gaunt had gone.

'What a bloody performance!' said Marsh, pulling the spectacles from his nose.

'There must have been an electrical storm,' said Swann. 'That's the only explanation. Or the ship was attacked by birds.' Who knew what horrors were hiding from men in the turbulent mountains of cloud? 'It's terrible. Terrible. He was a fine, brave man.'

'He was mad!' brayed Marsh.

'I'll not have you speak with so little respect for the dead!' shouted Swann, angry to find that his hands were shaking.

'A man must speak his mind,' returned Marsh. 'And he was a danger to himself and everyone he encountered.'

'He wanted to fly. He wanted to give men the gift of wings. He died like a British hero.'

'He broke his neck,' said Marsh, flatly. 'And he nearly managed to take you with him.'

Swann was invited to the funeral at Gaunt's beef gravy factory in Bristol. He bought a new set of mourning clothes and had a crepe ribbon stitched to his cap. Once Stanley Gaunt's bones were recovered they were rendered down to a fine black pepper and sealed in a crystal bottle. A priest held a service over the bottle and then it was placed in a niche twenty feet up in the factory wall and a tablet set in the stone. It was a very grand occasion. The workers had been given a holiday, with an extra sixpence in their wages, to mourn the death of the aviator. At the end of the day the guests were sent home with souvenir hymn books and complimentary bottles of gravy.

When driven by their enemies to defend such eccentric arrangements, the family announced that they thought the gravy works to be as close to a house of God as any regular church. The building had turned so much blood into money they reckoned it must be a miracle. God was surrounded by mystery but he'd clearly shown his fondness for gravy.

Swann was inclined to agree with them. The factory was like a cathedral with its vaulted ceilings and elaborate stained glass windows. The windows depicted *The Twenty Merits of Honest Labour* and the ceilings were buttoned with bosses, carved in the shape of bulls' heads. The crystal bottle displayed in its niche might well have contained the dust of some distant, foreign saint.

When Swann returned to London he felt exhausted and depressed. He couldn't concentrate on his work and closed the studio for a week. He had a photograph of the *Ostrich* mounted in a black silk frame and put on display in the window. He spent the days sitting quietly at home and tried to recover his spirits. But sometimes at night he dreamt he was falling, head over heels, through the boiling clouds that separated the earth from the heavens. The clouds would dissolve to reveal the rushing spires of London, thousands of broken and rusty swords, and then he would startle awake with a shout, his body spreadeagled on the mattress and his big beard spangled with sweat.

19

The following year Bleriot flew the English Channel.

'The aeroplane is at Selfridges,' said Marsh. 'They've put the machine on display in the store.'

'They'd make an exhibition from a monkey and a tattooed lady if they thought it would make 'em money,' said Swann.

'They say we'll soon be flying to France, regular as clockwork,' continued Marsh. 'The Channel steamers are finished.'

'I'm not interested!' shouted Swann impatiently.

'I am surprised,' grinned Marsh. 'And you so anxious to try your hand at aerial photography.' He enjoyed taunting the old man. It rankled that his master should be infatuated with something as dangerously modern as flight when he, himself, could not find the stomach for it. He had taken the news of Stanley Gaunt's death with all the bitter satisfaction of a man who has proved himself a prophet. He had known, all along, that it wouldn't work and it must only be a matter of time before the daft, French Bleriot broke his neck.

But Swann was cured of his interest in flight. It was the last time he looked to the future for inspiration. He ignored the news of Bleriot and devoted himself to his work.

He stalked the streets in search of fresh women to feed to the hungry camera. At the pawnbroker's shop in the Edgware Road he encountered a beauty with mocking eyes and employed her help in *The Judgement of Paris*. One evening, walking in Brewer Street, he found Susannah selling bowls of jellied eels to a crowd of beer-soaked Elders.

Every woman had something about her person that made her beautiful. He fell in love with their ears or their hands or the shape of their curving mouths. He adored their teeth, their dimpled knees or the colour of their nipples. A woman could hide nothing from his penetrating stare. He owned such a greatly experienced eye that he found he could measure their private parts at a glance, without so much as ruffling a feather.

His method of approach was simple: he stopped the women of his choice and asked them to pose for him. He compared them to works of art by famous, fancy foreigners, described them as a Greek or Roman goddess and begged permission to take their portraits. This frank approach at first amused and then intrigued them and led them, at last, to his studio. Swann looked so blissfully innocent and his old-fashioned clothes so peculiar that women never failed to be seduced by what, they supposed, must be an artist of genius. If modesty finally held them back he found that flattery, alone, could pull the laces from their corsets. They couldn't resist this huge, old bear in voluminous pantaloons.

He picked up Annie Potter in a florist's shop in Baker Street. She was a heavy, clumsy girl with brooding eyes and a plump, lascivious mouth. She looked ugly in her boots and apron but Swann could tell, at once, that he'd made an important discovery.

Marsh was dismayed when she first arrived at the studio. As far as he was any judge she looked as plain as a ha'penny loaf. But stepping out on the stage, without the disguise of her miserable clothes, she was found to be the most magnificent nude he had ever seen in his life. She was a voluptuous beauty with broad shoulders, generous hips and a waist that pinched her body into the shape of a violin. She wore her hair loose, falling in ringlets against her neck. Her breasts were round and set very high. Her skin was as white as moonlight and gave off the scent of heliotrope.

Dressed in her working clothes she had seemed dullwitted and hesitant but without them, walking the little stage, she moved with a splendid arrogance, concealing nothing from their gaze and even asking for some almond oil to put a shine on her whiskers.

We beg to inform our friends, Marsh wrote in the catalogue, of the latest astounding triumphs in the realm of artistic photography. A new set of scenes, only recently completed, depicting

Hagar the Concubine Anointing Herself for Abraham. No expense has been spared to bring the Old Testament back to life and the connoisseur will marvel at the strength and vitality of the scenes. The dusky slave is one-and-twenty, built very big and, once revealed in the undraped condition, is found to lack nothing but modesty. Here the viewer finds himself cast in the role of Abraham while Hagar, completing her beautification, prepares to excite his carnal desire. .

Also available: *A Christian Girl at the Roman Games* and *The Pharaoh's Dancing Daughter.*

We must caution the collector that all these historical illustrations are true to life in every respect and should be purchased by none but the most experienced voluptuary.

20

Towards the end of the year Swann was approached by Golden Beehive, a printing house in the Strand. The publishers wanted seventy plates to decorate a new cloth edition of a book called *The Fresh Air and Sun-Bath System*. The system, based largely on nude gymnastics, would be illustrated with photographs. Should the Swann studio prove satisfactory, there was work waiting on *The Body Beautiful* and several other titles. The publishers called it the Modern Woman's Art Library and since, as Violet had always maintained, 'art is not hairy', all the photographs would be retouched.

'I can't fathom it out,' said Swann, when he'd finished reading their instruction. 'If the books are purchased and studied by women, why paint out the short and curlies? What are they hoping to hide from the reader that can't be found in a bedroom mirror?'

'I suppose the sight of their own short and curlies must make 'em feel faint,' cackled Cromwell Marsh. 'Women is very fastidious creatures.'

'Why don't they leave them in their drawers?'

'You can't perform nude gymnastics in drawers!' protested Marsh.

'But it's not healthy,' insisted Swann. 'It gives a false impression. It makes grown women look like monstrous babies.'

'A woman is lewd until she's shorn and then she becomes a nude,' said Marsh.

'So much commotion over women's whiskers,' sighed Kingdom Swann. 'It's a wonder that women haven't taken to shaving.'

'What shall we do,' said Cromwell Marsh, 'when life imitates art?'

They chose little Ethel Spooner for *The Fresh Air and Sun-Bath*

System. She was small and bright and built like a dancer. She had also been blessed with a very dainty set of whiskers which she trimmed to a feather with a pair of scissors, to save Cromwell Marsh the strain to his eyes when it came to retouching the plates.

The authoress had provided a full set of pencil diagrams to guide them through the photographs. The Handstand. The Crab. The Vertical Swing. None of it looked difficult and the only equipment they needed to find was a metal climbing frame. It seemed like easy money.

For the first few chapters Ethel performed like an acrobat. She stretched and strutted and positively glowed with health. She walked on her hands and stood on her head. But towards the sixth chapter she was finding it hard to play the part of the laughing sunbeam. She grew sullen and clumsy and lost concentration. On the morning of the seventh set of exercises she arrived for work in great distress, pulled off her clothes and burst into tears.

It was several minutes before she found the breath to speak. Swann made her blow her nose. Marsh gave her sips of sweet brown sherry and a slice of sultana cake. Snuffling, choking, spitting crumbs, with her eyes burnt by mascara and her nose as raw as a radish, she managed, at last, to tell them her troubles.

She had been evicted from her room in Heaven's Yard. There had been no warning. The landlord had arrived and given her notice. She was frightened and confused. She didn't know where to turn for help.

'Why does he want you to leave?' asked Swann gently.

'It's the room, sir,' sobbed Ethel. 'He says it's terrible over-crowded.'

'How's that?' said Swann. He helped her wipe her nose with an end of the sodden handkerchief.

'I share it with my family, sir, and there's seven of us all together,' she sniffed.

'Seven in a room?' laughed Swann.

'None of us is very big,' scowled Ethel, 'and we takes it in turns to use the bed.'

'But that's impossible,' said Swann. He stopped laughing.

He turned to Cromwell Marsh for support. The story was preposterous. But Marsh, who was better informed of Ethel's unhappy circumstance, drained the last of the sherry and maintained a guilty silence.

'Perhaps you could stay with your elder sister,' Swann suggested kindly, taking her by the hand.

'No,' sobbed Ethel miserably. 'She doesn't want me.'

'Gloria has a room in Old Compton Street,' whispered Marsh, as if that explained everything.

'I'm sure she could manage until Ethel is settled again,' said Swann, failing to understand the problem.

'Her sister entertains gentlemen,' said Marsh confidentially. 'It wouldn't be decent for little Ethel to share the room. It's a dangerous predicament. The gentlemen is most particular...' He was about to say more but fell silent and picked at the hairs in his nostrils.

'Do you have no other connections?'

'None,' said Ethel.

'You could sleep here,' said Swann in desperation. He looked doubtfully around the studio.

'A lady needs her comforts,' objected Marsh. 'It's cold at night. It wouldn't suit.' He didn't want a woman getting under his feet or trying to fiddle with the dark-room plumbing.

Swann nodded and frowned and searched his pockets for aniseed balls. 'I'll take her home!' he said at last. It was an excellent idea. The house was huge. There were four empty bedrooms. It was a crime to let them go to waste.

'What would Violet say about that?' said Marsh darkly.

'She'll be delighted,' said Swann. 'Violet? She'll be thrilled to help a woman in distress. She's always talking about the plight of women. She's always quoting the sisterhood.'

'Does she work for a charity?' asked Ethel who feared, for a moment, that she might be sent to the workhouse.

'Bless you,' said Swann. 'You couldn't call it a charity.'

'Perhaps she works for the church,' said Ethel. She had a friend who lived in a Christian mission. They sang for their supper and slept with bibles under their beds. It wasn't much of a life but the food was hot and wholesome and the lodgings secure.

Swann shook his head. 'She's not what you'd call a God-fearing woman,' he said.

'God was a man!' roared Cromwell Marsh. He laughed loudly and pulled on his nose.

Ethel was looking confused. She felt the tears start to swell in her eyes and buried her face in the handkerchief.

'She's a suffragette,' confessed Swann. 'My housekeeper joined with the suffragettes.'

'She's a Millie!' chortled Cromwell Marsh.

Ethel was very impressed. 'I've seen them marching,' she said. 'Shouting at people and singing songs.'

'That's them,' said Marsh.

'Has she been to prison with Mrs Pankhurst?'

'No!' said Swann indignantly.

'It's her chief ambition,' said Marsh. 'Every time she meets a policeman she offers herself to the handcuffs. There's no promotion in the suffragettes until you've been under arrest. It's the only qualification. They want to attract the criminal classes to make their petticoat parliament.'

Swann ignored him. 'You'll like Violet,' he said. 'She'll do everything she knows to help. You'll have your own room, regular meals and all the comforts of home.'

Ethel wiped her eyes and smiled. Sitting, naked, on the edge of the stage she looked like a Fletcher-Whitby fairy. She was so slight you could see her bones. Her skin was very white, her hair as fine as eiderdown, her fingers and toes remarkably long and slender. But for the bumptious breasts she might have been taken for some pixilated child.

'Is it settled?'

'Yes,' said Ethel. 'Yes.' She was so excited she jumped from the stage and threw her arms around Swann's neck. The old man laughed and puffed out his beard.

Marsh wagged his head. 'There'll be trouble,' he muttered, clacking his teeth.

21

Swann left Marsh in the studio and followed Ethel to Poland Street where she took his hand and led him through the narrow lanes towards the room in Heaven's Yard. These cobbled tracks, cut deep as canals among the tenement buttresses, were denied any light from the sun. They were chilled and dark and running with gravy from broken drains. The buildings pressed down from every side, leaning together for support, their black walls bulging and covered with twisted flights of stairs that hung from the rooftops like cobwebs. Here and there a building had nearly been eaten away by the countless years of neglect and decay and, trapped by its neighbours with nowhere to collapse, had rotted into a skeleton. Swann was lost in this wasteland. He stumbled and tried to turn back but Ethel would not release him.

'Is it far?' he whispered, afraid that his voice would disturb the shadows.

'A little further down, sir,' she said.

The lane opened into a courtyard filled with smoke from a smouldering fire. A large man lay, facedown, in the ashes guarded by an idiot child. The child was tied to its owner's wrist by a length of rusty chain. Its face was badly bruised and one of its boots was missing. When Ethel and Swann tried to cross its path, the child grew alarmed, scampered around on its hands and knees, bared its teeth and barked.

'Is it far?' he whispered.

She squeezed the old man's hand and led him deeper into the lanes.

'A little further down, sir.'

The path grew darker, the ground beneath his feet erupting into pools of poisonous mud that splashed his legs and stank.

He had never strayed so far into hell nor believed that such hell existed. He would die here, lost in the maze, drowned in the filth that surrounded him.

At last, when he thought that all hope was lost, Ethel steered him through a small brick porch and up a flight of stairs. These stairs, broken and buckled on their foundations, were full of cats and squatting children. A stew of smells assaulted him. Sour mutton, urine, cabbage, beer, sweat and unwashed rags. Behind locked doors there were babies bawling. Somewhere beneath them a woman was screaming.

They continued to climb through the darkness until Swann groaned aloud and felt his knees bending under him. The effort had proved too much for his heart. His legs were soft as rubber and he couldn't organise his feet. Is this how it must end, dropping dead in a den of thieves, gold watch stolen, corpse carried off for the student surgeons? He was seized with such fear that he burst his collar. His head was wobbling in its socket.

'It's no good,' he wheezed, falling down in a heap and clutching at his pounding heart. 'I'm finished!'

'Don't worry, sir,' said Ethel, standing beside an open door. 'This one, here, is my address. We've arrived.'

Swann, feeling foolish, nervously picked himself up and hobbled quickly into the room.

There was a metal bed, a table and chair and a cupboard that served as a wardrobe. An old blanket had been hung against the window, reducing the room to a dismal twilight. A paraffin lamp cast its glow on the table and, at the table, sat an old woman and five, small, silent children. They were making dolls from clothes-pegs. Some of the children painted the pegs while others cut skirts from paper scraps. The mother added the faces with a tiny hogs'-hair brush. The eyes and the mouth: two dots and a dash. They didn't stop work for Kingdom Swann but gave him a glance and ignored him. Once the faces were finished and the paper skirts fitted with a dab of glue, the dolls were pegged on lines to dry. The lines stretched beneath the ceiling like a jumble of telegraph wires.

Ethel approached the old woman and tenderly kissed her cheek. Then she kissed each child, in turn, and introduced

Kingdom Swann as a gentleman philanthropist.

The woman, who seemed to be out of her wits, laughed at this news and offered to sell him her children. 'Have this one!' she said, cuffing the nearest boy and knocking the scissors from his hand. 'There's more fat on him. Some of the others are skin and bone!' Then she fell silent and continued working with the brush as if nothing at all had happened. Two dots and a dash. Two dots and a dash.

Swann retreated into a corner and waited for Ethel to collect her belongings. Two dots and a dash. No one spoke again. He looked at the five tiny children working, tongues stuck out in concentration, snot hanging down from button noses, and the scene began to fill him with horror. It wasn't the work that shocked him, nor even the squalor of their surroundings, but the meaningless drudgery of their labour! They had been reduced to primitive automatons, dead to the world, triggered into mechanical movement. How could they live to such little purpose, deprived of fresh air and sunlight? How did they manage to survive in this morbid state of stupefaction? He wanted to shout at them, run forward, shake them awake and lead them into the daylight world. But he was a stranger in a foreign land and could do no more than stand and stare.

After a few minutes he became aware of someone watching him through a crack in the door. He stepped forward and pulled the door open. A neat little man with a shaved head swaggered slowly into the room. He wore a velvet suit, drenched in the scent of frangipani and in one small, immaculate hand he carried a bunch of iron keys.

The man cocked an eyebrow at Swann and studied him for another full minute, paying great attention to the old man's nose, as if he were viewing a circus attraction.

'Do I suppose, sir, that you're acquainted with this young baggage?' he said at last, smiling at Swann and waving the bunch of keys at Ethel.

'Well acquainted, sir!' growled Swann, puffing out his beard.

'And do I suppose you've come to take said baggage away?'

'Yes!' snapped Swann, 'Since you leave me no choice in the matter.'

The landlord beamed with pleasure and shook Swann by the hand, as if it were reason for jolliment. 'My warmest congratulations! No hard feelings, I trust. I wouldn't want her to walk the street but it's all a matter of hygiene. Old women cause me no trouble and no more do God's little children. Widows and orphans, sir. Widows and orphans. It's the young women cause the heartache.' He looked at Ethel and shuddered. 'To tell the truth I can't abide 'em. When they're not fighting they're stealing and when they're not stealing they're spawning. They give clean lodgings a most unsavoury reputation.'

This seemed remarkably squeamish for a man who let rooms in such a hovel but Swann was in no mood to argue with him. Ethel had already packed and said goodbye to the half-witted clothes-peg family. Her luggage did not amount to more than a bag of clothes, two pairs of boots, a coronation mug, a little mirror in a seashell frame and a very tattered vulture-quill hat.

'You're a rum old dog,' grinned the landlord as he followed them into the passage. 'But I've no doubt a fresh young baggage can teach you a few new tricks. And once you've had your fun and frolics she'll earn you a pretty penny.'

Swann glared at the landlord. His face was black with rage and a rush of blood inflated his nose. He turned upon the unfortunate man and let out a roar that burst in the air like a thunderstorm. 'May you burn in the fires of hell, sir!' he bellowed. Despite his great age and his tremulous bulk he could still strike fear into men with a shout. When he let it rip he could shatter coal and knock a child dead at twenty paces. It was a deep and penetrating bark that punched the stuffing from his opponents and shocked the world into silence.

The landlord flung himself at the wall and tried to stifle a whimper.

'Are you ready?' said Swann, turning to Ethel.

'I'm ready,' she whispered.

He bundled her thankfully down the stairs and hurried her home towards Golden Square. She would have the big bedroom with the Chinese curtains, a good hot bath every morning and four square meals a day. She would have new frocks, silk drawers, the best of everything.

22

Violet Askey received the refugee in the drawing room and, while she served sweet tea and toast, Swann talked about their adventures.

'You could never imagine such hell!' he said. 'How can anything but disease be expected to flourish in those conditions? It's a national disgrace. We saw infants so pale they must never have seen God's light of day. Dozens of 'em in a bed that they share with the lice and the vermin. People so wretched and poor they'd cut your throat for a sixpence. We saw such sights that would curdle your blood and give you nightmares for the rest of your life.'

Ethel sat on the edge of her chair, desperately clutching a bone china cup. She didn't have the courage to drink. She sat before Violet, frozen with fright, and studied a distant dangle of grapes in the brilliance of the stained glass windows.

'A disgrace!' concluded Swann. He was flushed with indignation. He couldn't convey the smell, the noise, the horror of it.

The housekeeper listened in silence. She was staring at Ethel with hard, unblinking eyes. A blue vein twitched in her temple. When Swann had finished his address he told Violet to take their guest to the room with the Chinese curtains.

'Provide her with every comfort,' he shouted after them. 'She's been the victim of constant neglect. We must see that she wants for nothing.'

'I hope you'll make yourself at home,' Violet said crisply, as she led the unfortunate girl upstairs. 'We shall dine at eight o'clock tonight. I trust you find that convenient. We are, naturally, at your beck and call.'

Ethel dropped a curtsey. She was so intimidated she spent

the rest of the day in her room, perched on a chair in her vulture-quill hat.

At dinner she could not touch the food. She seemed alarmed by the starched linen and the sparkling silver, the glow of electric candlesticks, the tiny, hand-written menu cards, the elaborate etiquette employed to spoon a pudding. Violet had spared no pains in the kitchen to create a long and difficult supper.

'You poor child, I was told you were starving,' she murmured as she served her guest with a large, boiled trout.

The fish stared blindly at Ethel with an eye cooked into a milky blister and dared her to disturb its bones. Ethel looked to Swann for help but the old man was falling asleep, his hands loose, his face sinking into his pillow of beard. It had been a long day and he'd lost all his appetite for food. His nose was still haunted by the stink of the rooms in Heaven's Yard. So she sat at the table, embarrassed and silent, with Violet standing at her shoulder, until Swann woke up with a snuffle and grunt.

'What?' he shouted. 'What?' He swept the napkin from his lap and stared in surprise at his plate. 'It's a damn fish!'

'They're very wholesome,' said Violet. 'I thought you'd welcome the nourishment.'

'Take it away,' said Swann in disgust, prodding the article with his fork.

The housekeeper stepped forward and reluctantly removed the offending corpses.

'I never liked fish,' grumbled Swann as soon as she'd left the room. 'We'll ask her to cook an omelette.'

But Ethel had already jumped from her chair and was running upstairs to safety.

23

'How could you do this to me?' screeched Violet. It was late. Ethel was safe in her soft, silk bed.

'I thought you'd be pleased to help,' said Swann. He was sitting at the table, hunched across a bowl of apples. It felt cold in the room. The fire in the grate was a heap of ashes. He picked up a little silver knife and tapped it impatiently against his fingers. 'The poor girl is destitute.'

'The word is prostitute!' snapped Violet.

'Ethel Spooner is a most respectable young lady,' said Swann, very shocked.

'You wouldn't recognise a lady if she walked up to you in the street and slapped your face,' said Violet. She marched around the table, clipping the chairs with her billowing skirts.

'What harm has she done you, madam?' demanded Swann. 'I thought you'd make her welcome in my house. You're always talking about the sisterhood of women.'

'And I suppose you thought I'd be happy to have my home filled by your ten-shilling whores?' she shouted.

'Hush! You'll wake the street.'

'I don't care if I wake the dead,' shouted Violet. 'You're deliberately trying to humiliate me. You just don't seem to understand. You have no idea of the suffering of women!' Her face was red and her eyes were filling with tears.

'Ethel is a woman!' roared Kingdom Swann. 'Ethel is suffering!' He grabbed the knife and began to stab at a large, green apple. The skin hissed fragrant bubbles.

'I forbid you to keep a prostitute.'

'She is not a prostitute and I refuse to turn her out in the street.' He scowled at the ruined fruit, pulled out the knife and wiped the blade on his thumb.

'This is intolerable. I demand that you tell her to leave.'

'No, madam! I shall not be bullied by my own housekeeper and there's an end to it.'

'Is that your last word?'

'Yes.'

'May God forgive you, Kingdom Swann.'

'Where are you going?'

'I'm going to bed. And tomorrow I'm leaving this wicked house. I hope you and your strumpet burn in hell!'

The next morning Violet cooked breakfast but left them to serve it for themselves. Ethel took advantage of the house-keeper's absence by stuffing herself with porridge and kippers, boiled eggs and hot muffins. When Swann took her down to the studio she was so bloated she could barely breathe. It was the first time in weeks that she hadn't felt hungry.

Cromwell Marsh was burning with curiosity about Ethel's reception at the house of the bestial virgin, but a glance from the master made him bite his tongue.

'Did you ever visit Heaven's Yard?' Swann inquired abruptly, as they settled down to work.

'I never actually went there in person,' said Marsh.

'I recommend it,' said Swann and nothing more was mentioned.

Ethel took off her clothes and began her pandiculations. They made good progress and, by the end of the afternoon, *The Fresh Air and Sun-Bath System* was very nearly complete. Marsh was left alone to begin the laborious task of developing the plates. Swann took Ethel back to Golden Square.

'You're so kind,' she said, as they walked reluctantly home through the twilight. 'If it wasn't for you I don't know where I should sleep tonight.'

'It's a pleasure,' said Swann.

'I've been so wretched,' Ethel confessed. 'There were times when I wanted to finish it and throw myself in the river.'

'Don't think about it!' shuddered Swann. He could picture Ethel afloat in the Thames, her skirts fanned out in the oily water, her drowned face pale and beautiful. 'Don't think such terrible thoughts!'

'Do you think your housekeeper likes me?' she ventured as they entered Glasshouse Street and found themselves approaching the Square. She was beginning to look distinctly unhappy.

'Why do you ask?' growled Swann. 'What's happened? Has she said something to upset you?'

'Oh, no,' Ethel said quickly.

'You mustn't take any notice of Violet,' he said. 'She feels unsettled with strangers. We lead a very quiet life. But she'll soon improve when she gets to know you.'

'She's such a grand lady,' said Ethel. 'Is she really in league with the suffragettes?'

'I believe they've won her sympathies,' he said. 'You know, they're working for great reforms.'

'But they do such terrible mischief,' said Ethel, taking his arm to guide him safely through the traffic.

'And it's terrible how they're treated,' said Swann. 'The world is changing so fast. I can't pretend to understand it.'

When they reached the house they found a motor-cab parked at the door. The driver, sitting aboard the machine, was patiently sucking a short clay pipe. He tipped his hat and winked at Ethel.

'You've got company,' said Ethel in dismay. She thought of another difficult dinner, the elaborate table, the problem of so many knives and spoons. She felt sick. She wanted to turn and run away.

'I'm not receiving,' said Swann defiantly. He scowled at the cabbie and pulled on the bell.

The front door swung open to reveal a tall woman in a horse-hair wig and a black velvet coat. She was surrounded by trunks and boxes. Swann recognised the luggage. It belonged to his housekeeper.

'Who are you?' he said.

'You rascal!' shouted the woman. 'You dirty dog! You devil!' And she hit him with her handbag.

Ethel screamed. Swann fell down and cracked his head on the floor. His assailant, flatulent with indignation, towered above him and threatened him with her fists.

Violet came running down the stairs in a flurry of feathers and furs. 'You've met Mrs Nottingham,' she said, finding her master on the floor. She didn't look surprised. She stepped over him and beckoned the cabbie into the house.

'Where are you going, madam?' demanded Swann, struggling to his feet. The cabbie, his pipe tucked behind one ear, began wrestling the luggage down to the street.

'Mrs Nottingham has a shelter for the independent woman,' said Violet.

'Shelter?' shrieked Swann. 'You're already living in the lap of luxury, tucked away in this damn great house with nothing to do with your time but make mischief.'

'She is going to a *safe* house,' boomed Mrs Nottingham. 'The victim of a rich man's whim.'

'I'll thank you to shut your mouth!' said Kingdom Swann.

'No more! The women of this country have been silent for too long!' she bellowed. Her eyes blazed and she'd grown a moustache of perspiration. She was clearly enjoying herself. 'It's our turn to speak. It's our turn to cry for justice. We shall have our liberty. We shall cast off our shackles. And, when the time comes, we shall bring this government to its knees. I'm not afraid of you. I've thrown stones at Lloyd George.' She bent down and hit him again with her handbag.

'You've stolen my housekeeper!'

'Stolen? Why, she's no more to you than a runaway slave.'

'I've treated her like a sister,' said Swann.

'Is this how you treat a sister?' shouted Mrs Nottingham, pointing her finger at Ethel. 'Forcing her to conspire in your sinister debaucheries?'

'What?' groaned Swann, rubbing his head and turning to plead with Violet. 'Why don't you tell her the truth of it?'

Violet snorted, turned away and swept majestically into the street.

'And *you*, miserable wretch, what have you to say for yourself?' demanded Mrs Nottingham, turning on Ethel as the sweating cabbie removed the last trunk.

'Leave her alone,' said Swann. He was bruised and angry and losing his patience. 'The poor girl is frightened to death.'

'Has she a tongue in her head?'

'She doesn't have to answer to you.'

'Let her speak,' said Mrs Nottingham.

Ethel, who had been trying to hide behind a chair, tottered forward, jerked back her head and puked on Mrs Nottingham's skirt.

24

S wann thought of hiring a manservant, someone to care for his boots and collars, but Ethel wouldn't hear of it. She wanted to play at housekeeper and wore a uniform she thought suitable for such a lofty position, strutting about in an afternoon dress, sensible shoes and a frilled cap, smiling at herself in mirrors. It was the first time in her life she had found work that required clothes.

Despite Swann's protests, she moved from the room with the Chinese curtains and settled herself in the attic. He tried to talk her down but she seemed so happy and comfortable that he let her stay in the servants' quarters. In the beginning he had his doubts about her household duties. There was so much work to be done and he still regarded her as his guest.

'I'm used to hard work,' she insisted, whenever he suggested she might like some help around the place. 'And we don't want the house full of strangers.'

It suited Swann. Ethel was a genius in the kitchen, stewing beef and boiling ham, and neither of them cared a farthing for the cobwebs that hung from the chandeliers or the dust that rolled on the stairs.

'Leave the dust to grow until it's long enough to cut with shears,' he advised and Ethel was most obedient.

When he came home in the evenings she was waiting for him with hot beef puddings which they ate together, below stairs, by the warmth of the Livingstone range.

The old house seemed to sigh with relief to be spared the broom and the scrubbing brush. It felt comfortable as it grew dishevelled. Ethel didn't care for regular cleaning and most of the rooms settled down to a sooty slumber.

Cromwell Marsh, who had long been forbidden to visit, was

invited home once a month for supper. Sometimes he brought
Ethel's sister and she, in turn, brought Gladys Pickles, who had
found some success, at last, as a dancer and came to the house
with a string of admirers.

Lord Hugo Prattle came to call, whenever his business
brought him to London and, although Ethel would polish the
dining room table and make an effort to clean the best silver, he
always wanted to eat in the kitchen, happy and sweating beside
the range, with his braces down and his boots unlaced.

Swann often thought of Violet and wondered how she was
passing her time. He never understood her anger or forgave her
disapproval of Ethel. But he felt sad, because he loved her none
the less, and worried about her safety in the world beyond
Golden Square. Whenever the suffragettes marched he
searched for her name in the evening paper, dreading he'd find
her listed among the women arrested or injured.

Once when out walking, between Dover Street and Berkeley
Square, he thought he had seen her with another woman, wearing a suffragette apron and a canvas satchel full of posters. He
knew it was Violet by the tilt of her head and the confident way
she carried herself although, later, he couldn't have sworn to it.
She looked so different out of uniform. He followed her for
several minutes but she vanished, at last, among the crowds in
the Burlington Arcade.

It was bad to have lost a housekeeper but, at night, when the
kitchen was full of laughter, the steam spurting from the big
kettle, the oven full of fragrant puddings, Prattle honking at
Marsh dancing as the girls sat singing at the long, scrubbed
table, he was glad to have found such a family of friends.

25

'And you say she eloped with another woman?' said Mrs Beeton over afternoon tea.

'Stolen from under my nose, ma'am,' said Swann. 'When I reached home that night she was already packed and preparing to leave my service.' He paused to bite a coconut cake and tidy his beard with a napkin. 'You grow very fond of a person when you've lived with them for the best part of fifteen years,' he reflected bitterly.

'Shocking,' said Mrs Beeton. 'And you've heard nothing since?'

'Nothing,' said Swann. 'It's as if she evaporated. But I've every reason to believe that she's hiding with the suffragettes. '

'They're mischievous times, Mr Swann,' said Mrs Beeton.

'I wouldn't want her to come to harm,' said Swann. 'She was always an independent woman and we often had our disagreements but she did what she could to comfort me.'

'Comfort, Mr Swann?' said Mrs Beeton quietly, arching a perfectly painted eyebrow.

'When Mrs Swann was taken from me,' he explained. 'A solace, madam, in my time of grief.'

Mrs Beeton nodded wisely. 'I've been put to grief myself, sir. My husband was a nincompoop but he was my husband, for all that, and I missed him when he was gone.'

'I married in '73,' said Swann. 'The year of the great Ashanti war. I was nearly fifty years old and she no more than a girl. These days people would think it a scandal. And yet we were happy together. She was everything a man might hope for in a wife.'

'And you a most indulgent husband,' said Mrs Beeton, to flatter him.

'Ah, but she was a lovely creature,' said Swann. 'She had so much energy and grace. She was delicate, of course, but I did what I could to protect her from an extreme of excitement. She had eyes of a penetrating blue – that was her chief attraction – and a very pretty laugh that exposed a perfect set of teeth, although that came as no surprise since her father was a dentist. But I've never known a woman with such a loving tempera- ment. I do declare, she would have made an excellent mother. Children were her great delight and yet, it's cruel how we were denied them.'

'A mixed blessing,' said Mrs Beeton coldly. 'I can't abide 'em myself although, I dare say, there's some women can find a sort of pleasure in them. Why, there are women I've seen so wretched and poor a child is the only thing they may honestly call their own; yet I don't see how it brings 'em comfort. A sick man might be said to own his disease but he'd be happier with- out it.'

'That's a very harsh judgement, ma'am,' said Swann.

'There's many things we need in this world, Mr Swann,' said Mrs Beeton. 'More dogs and more children ain't two of them. And besides, it wouldn't suit a girl here to have infants clinging to her skirts while there's still so many grown men require nurs- ing.'

'I've no regrets for myself, ma'am, but I know *she* dreamed of a family,' said Swann. He paused, chasing a strand of coconut with his tongue.

'Do you have a picture, sir?' said Mrs Beeton, seizing the opportunity to cut short his song of praise. It wasn't the first time in her life that a man had felt moved in her company to describe the virtues of his wife, although it usually took some- thing stronger than a cup of tea and a cake.

Kingdom Swann abandoned his plate and fumbled about in his pockets. After some struggling he produced a miniature, painted on an ivory flake and kept in a little purse, saturated with the smell of aniseed.

'Charming,' said Mrs Beeton. It was an unremarkable picture of an ordinary young woman with an open, friendly face and a piece of ribbon tied through her hair.

'It was my last attempt to paint,' confided Swann. 'When we were married I was already trying to earn my living as the worst kind of portrait photographer.'

'And you never felt tempted to put your wife before the camera?' asked Mrs Beeton in surprise.

Swann scowled and looked uncomfortable. 'I must confess I never thought a machine could capture the essence of so much beauty. How could you hope to squeeze such visions through a hole in a cheap wooden box? It didn't make sense. And I wasn't alone in that belief. There were many great men who agreed with me.'

'And yet this was your last painted work,' said Mrs Beeton, returning the portrait.

'Despite myself, I came to believe that the art of painting was dead,' said Kingdom Swann sadly. He gazed for a moment at his wife before slipping her into his pocket. 'A man with a camera could photograph the population of a small town in the time it required to paint one portrait. No artist could hope to compete with the speed of such a machine. It was terrible. There were suicides. You could buy a studio for a song.'

'It was a very difficult time.'

'Difficult?' growled Swann. 'It was a tragedy!'

'And yet the old art survived,' said Mrs Beeton, waving her hand about the room with considerable satisfaction. She had recently purchased some pencil drawings by a dwarf called Toulouse-Lautrec who had lived and worked in a Paris brothel. She was thinking of finding her own artist to live at the Villa Arcadia. The idea tickled her fancy.

'Yes. Painting survived the photograph and these days you need a sharp pair of eyes to tell the two apart. But at the time I felt differently.'

'And now?'

'I have nothing but regrets. I wish I'd shown her to the camera. There's something about a photograph I'd describe as supernatural. It's the mysterious preservation of an individual's shadow. Why, it's as much a part of a person as a fingerprint or a locket of hair. No one who sits for the camera will ever completely die for they go on living in their photographs.'

'Perhaps I should sit for my own portrait, sir, for I'm feeling my age in the bones,' said Mrs Beeton and laughed and rang the bell for another kettle of water.

26

The following year Kingdom Swann was eighty-five and to mark his birthday Ethel planned a special family supper. But a fortnight before the celebration the King dropped dead and Swann felt obliged to cancel the arrangements.

'It seems a shame,' said Ethel, rather wistfully. 'Gladys promised a song and dance and I've ordered a cake from Fortnum and Mason.'

It was too hot for funerals. The Thames stank and the streets had baked in the sulphurous sunlight. Yet despite the weather the city turned out to watch the parade as it passed on its way to Windsor. The people shuffled forth in their thousands, from every house and hovel, factory and sweat-shop; clinging to railings and hanging from statues, climbing, one upon another, in their bid for a glimpse of the royal coffin, until the streets were overflowing and the people were fainting from heat and excitement.

Marsh and Swann, in their Sunday black, jostled for position on the crowded pavement while Ethel, between them, stood stretching on tiptoe, wrinkling her nose at the ripe smell of soldiers, leather, horse dung and countless mothballed mourning gowns.

'He didn't last long, God bless him,' said Marsh, snapping to attention as the gun carriage went creaking past. He snatched off his hat and held it lightly over his heart.

'There's the new King,' said Swann suddenly, waving at a group of horsemen.

'Where?' cried Ethel. The crowd surged and knocked her down. She jumped to her feet, breathless and laughing, and smacked at the dust on her sleeves.

'There!' shouted Swann, 'The one riding with the German Kaiser.'

The Kaiser, astride a great, white horse, turned for a moment and looked down on Ethel. A fountain of feathers poured from his hat and his chest was blazing with planets and stars.

'The new King!' blushed Ethel, clapping her hands in delight. 'The new King and he smiled at me!'

'And Lord Kitchener – I think I saw Lord Kitchener!' hooted Marsh, who seemed very much impressed.

'And there's Lord Roberts,' said Swann, pointing a finger at a cloud of dust.

'And King What's-his-name!' said Marsh, searching all the sweating faces.

'I never dreamed there was so much royalty in the world!' cried Ethel happily.

The funeral turned at the corner of the street and the crowd exploded, rushing forward to chase the retreating horses. Someone caught Swann's coat in the scramble and tried, half-heartedly, to steal his gold watch. Ethel was tripped and fell down again.

'Are you hurt?' shouted Swann, as he bravely tried to shelter her from the onslaught of the mob.

'I think I've torn my stockings,' she wailed, feeling under her skirt for her knees.

'We'll all die in this crush – let's go home!' shouted Swann, grabbing at Ethel's hand and trying to lead her to safety.

They reached the shelter of a draper's doorway before they realised they had lost Cromwell Marsh.

'Where's he gone?' sobbed Ethel. She was bruised and frightened and sick with heat.

'That's him!' said Swann, peering anxiously into the crowd. 'What's happened? Someone is trying to murder him!'

He pushed out from the doorway towards Cromwell Marsh who was caught in the clutch of a very large woman. The woman was so tall, and was shaking him so hard, that his feet had left the ground. He dangled from her arms like a poorly stuffed rag doll.

'Oh, my Gawd, it's him!' she moaned as Swann tried to step between them. She dropped Marsh who fell in the gutter where a child kicked his hat through the yellow puddles of dung.

'Quick!' muttered Swann, helping restore the printer's balance. 'Let's get away. The royalty must have gone to her head.'

'You don't understand!' shouted Marsh. He ran to retrieve his hat but lost it under a carriage.

'You're the very ghost of Kingdom Swann, the late lamented photographer,' sobbed the stranger. She was a handsome woman, about fifty years old, with a face that was sunburnt and mottled with dust. She was wearing a mourning suit and a bent bonnet wrapped in crepe. She seemed grief-stricken by the sight of the ancient photographer and stuffed her knuckles into her mouth.

'Who is this woman?' demanded Swann.

'Alice Hancock,' said Cromwell Marsh. 'You must remember Alice.'

'No.'

'That's because she's upset on account of the maudlin circumstance,' explained Marsh. 'Alice was very close to the King. He was partial to her personage.'

'You mean…' said Swann.

'Probably,' said Marsh.

'I don't remember,' said Swann. He frowned at the woman and shook his head.

'There's no reason you should remember,' said Marsh. 'I'm talking of times when he was only the Prince of Wales.'

'He might have been the Prince of Wales but he always behaved like a proper gent,' sobbed Alice. She began to sink beneath the weight of so much misery and Marsh had to lend his support. She gave a terrible groan, rolled her eyes and threatened to faint in his arms.

'She's looking very queer,' said Swann.

'It's the heat. I think she's been roaming the streets. The funeral must have hit her hard. She always loved the King.'

'Perhaps we should take her home,' said Swann gallantly.

'Good idea,' said Marsh. 'A glass of water, an easy chair and she'll soon be as right as ninepence.'

So they collected Ethel, who was still hiding in the draper's doorway, and helped Alice Hancock back to the house near Golden Square.

It wasn't until they had guided her down the stairs to the kitchen and propped her safely in a chair that she found the strength to speak again.

'Is he still here?' she whispered, holding Cromwell Marsh by the sleeve.

'Who?'

'The late Mr Swann.'

'I'm here,' said Swann, sloshing brandy into a glass.

'You're in his house,' said Marsh proudly.

'Is that right?' she said, peering about the room.

'Don't you remember what happened?' said Swann. 'We found you in the street. Your mind had started to wander.'

Alice groaned. 'You mustn't mind a poor woman, Mr Swann,' she said, gulping down the brandy. 'I was very close to the King. He was good to me.' She gasped as the brandy set fire to her throat.

'Mr Swann was good to you, Alice, don't forget. You was his favourite Jezebel, that's what he called you.'

'I was a beauty in my day,' agreed Alice, wiping the tears from her eyes. 'Wilkie Collins wrote me love letters.'

'You was famous for it,' said Marsh.

Alice nodded happily. 'Baron Leighton wanted to paint me. Can you believe it? He took me to his house in Holland Park Road. Poor old Fred! He was then so feeble he couldn't hold a brush. But he was stubborn. Oh, he was stubborn! He wanted me for his *Bath of Psyche*.'

'He used that actress, Dorothy Dene, for the *Bath of Psyche*,' said Kingdom Swann.

'Yes,' said Alice. 'And she was a great, long streak of nothing.' She took off her bonnet and shook out a mane of coarse, red hair. 'He was never happy with that painting, although they call it a masterpiece. The day we were introduced he said, Alice, my girl, I'm going to have you in my *Bath*. And he would have done too, if he'd been spared…'

Swann refilled her brandy glass.

'And don't forget Aubrey Beardsley,' prompted Marsh.

Alice snorted. 'He wanted to sketch me, dirty little man. I never liked him. He got mixed up in a lot of trouble. He chased me all over London. It gave me the creeps.'

'I can remember the days when you were the toast of the town,' said Marsh. 'There wasn't an artist alive who didn't covet your bum.'

'It's true,' nodded Alice humbly. 'But you were the one, 'she said, turning to Swann. 'Your photographs was lovely. Look, here, I'll show you.'

She plunged a hand between her breasts and hauled out a large, silver locket. The locket broke open to reveal a coloured photograph. A picture of Alice, wearing nothing but boots, looking fat and pink as a Botticelli.

'It's a cheerful view,' whistled Cromwell Marsh. 'I coloured you with my own hands. It seems like only yesterday. '

'Eighteen hundred and ninety-nine,' sighed Alice.

'I don't believe it!' gasped Marsh. 'Why, you're just as lovely now as you were when the portrait was taken. Indeed, I'd say you was lovelier, if a man may still trust his eyes.'

While they sat gawking at this masterpiece, Ethel made them a cold supper of sausage and pickle which they ate at the kitchen table. The company laughed and ate and drank and talked of the good old days. Ethel said nothing. She didn't feel easy with Alice Hancock, who was old enough to be her mother. She felt ignored and out of sorts. She sat with them for an hour or two more, opened a second bottle of brandy, slipped away and went to bed.

By midnight the brandy had driven Alice into another fit of despair. She sprawled in her chair and counted her sorrows. 'Freddy gone. Teddy gone. Everyone gone or going. What's to become of the likes of me?'

Swann was too drunk to offer advice. But Marsh waved his hand in protest. 'You're a feast for the eyes, Alice. It's not finished yet. Have some more brandy.'

'You're both so kind,' burbled Alice. 'You bring me home and you give me supper and it's more than enough to break my poor heart.'

'Stuff and nonsense!' shouted Marsh, splashing brandy over his shirt and soaking himself to the skin. 'Why, you could still show Swann a trick or two, eh? Yes! You knew how to transport yourself. You knew how to strike an attitude. You always had such nice big legs.'

'They have been admired,' agreed Alice. She belched and hoicked up her skirts.

'They're beauties!' growled Cromwell Marsh.

'I'm still fit and healthy,' said Alice.

'I should say you're in the prime of life!'

Her spirits rose with his flattery and she tried out a little dance. 'I could have been on the stage,' she laughed.

'Look at that!' crooned Marsh. 'Don't it set your blood on fire to see such a pair of big, fat knees!'

Swann lifted his head but found that he couldn't open his eyes so he grinned, instead, and silently slipped from his chair.

When he woke up it was morning. The kitchen was cold and deserted. Someone had covered him with a blanket and placed a pillow under his head. He lay quietly on the flagstones, trying to make sense of his strange surroundings and then, deciding that he hadn't died, struggled to his feet and endeavoured to climb the stairs.

When he reached the hall he found Cromwell Marsh slumped, asleep, with his head against the front door. He was snoring. His teeth had worked loose and his boots were missing.

Alice Hancock lay on her back in the middle of the carpet. She was wearing nothing but her silver locket and a pair of very old satin drawers. The drawers, which were trimmed with gold lace, bore a richly embroidered crest. Alice groaned. The sun as it soaked through a stained glass window, licked red and green and yellow shadows over her capsized breasts. Her stomach rolled and rumbled in slumber. Her mouth was open. She was blowing bubbles.

Swann knelt down and tried to shake Marsh awake. 'What happened here?' he whispered fiercely, pulling at his ear.

'We was dancing,' moaned Marsh, as he came back to life. His voice was thick and glued with sleep.

'What have you done to her clothes?'

'I don't remember,' said Marsh. He stood up and frowned at Alice. He took out his teeth and wiped them on the front of his shirt.

'How did she come to be dressed in a pair of Mrs Beeton's special edition royal drawers?' demanded Swann.

Cromwell Marsh blinked and pushed several fingers into his mouth. He seemed to have trouble fitting his teeth. 'I always bring 'em out for royal weddings and funerals,' he confessed at last. 'I likes the feel of 'em in my pocket.'

'But how did Alice come by them?'

'I wanted her to try 'em for size,' Marsh said apologetically. 'When she started dancing and kicking her legs I couldn't help myself.'

'Well, take her upstairs and put her to bed,' hissed Swann. 'She can't stay down here, she'll give Ethel a fright.'

Marsh tottered over to the sleeping woman, bent down and buried his hands in her armpits.

'She's too fat for me,' he wheezed. 'She'll do me a mischief.'

'You take her arms and I'll take her feet,' whispered Swann. He seized her by the ankles, raised her legs against his chest and tried to drive her, like a wheelbarrow, across the carpet.

A key grated in the lock and the front door opened. When Swann turned around he saw Violet Askey standing, framed in sunlight, dressed in a coat and a wide-brimmed hat. She stood, motionless, staring in horror, a little parcel strung on her wrist.

He was astonished. He laughed. But he could not move. He was still holding Alice Hancock's feet.

'Violet?' he said.

'Mr Swann?' said Violet, reaching her hand towards him.

'But…' he said.

'Happy birthday,' she said and let the parcel fall from her wrist and slap against the floor.

He dropped Alice Hancock and ran toward the retreating housekeeper. 'Wait!' he shouted. 'You don't understand!'

Alice Hancock woke up with a shout and shrank away from Cromwell Marsh. 'Who are you?' she shouted.

'Shut up!' snapped Marsh.

Swann followed Violet down the steps and onto the hot and dusty street. But the housekeeper would not wait for him. She was running, shouting, pleading for help, in a fury of flapping petticoats. Several men stopped and pointed at Swann. An old woman threw a stone at him. Violet reached the street corner and he was forced, at last, to give up the chase. His head was ringing and he couldn't catch his breath. He watched her dart through the dangerous traffic, jump aboard a motor bus and disappear in a cloud of smoke.

'Happy birthday,' said Marsh sadly, when Swann came hobbling back to the house. He was wearing a dirty tablecloth. Alice was dressed in his shirt.

Swann picked up the parcel and unwrapped a little book. It was *Health, Beauty and the New Vegetarian* by the Golden Beehive Press.

27

Alice Hancock stayed in the house near Golden Square. She had been living as a scullery-maid with a family in Kilburn but she never returned there to collect her clothes nor ask for a farthing of wages.

'Let the buggers find another skivvy,' was all she said to Swann. 'It's a life that's not worth the living, sir. You're up before dawn to light the fires and you don't see your bed before midnight. When you're not dusting and waxing and scrubbing and washing, you're peeling and cutting and boiling and baking. And when that's finished there's the boots to polish, the grates to black, the knives to shine, not to mention the running and fetching and the Missus complaining every five minutes and the Master wanting to feel your person.' She took a deep breath and shivered with disgust. She was finished with slaving for the *hoi polloi* and if she had to skivvy for someone she would rather skivvy for Swann. It was her intention to hide in the house and devote herself to his service.

'I wouldn't want you to work,' he said gravely, when she explained this plan. It was unthinkable. She was an educated woman and, despite her second-hand mourning clothes, still carried herself like a duchess. She was fierce and proud and independent and only the ugly red hands betrayed her years as a scullery-maid.

'Work for you, Mr Swann?' cried Alice. 'I'd think it an honour to slave for you, sir, and that's the honest truth!'

'But you came to the house as my guest. It wouldn't be decent to have you beat carpets.'

'You picked me out of the gutter, sir, when I was near mad with grief. You took me home and cared for me and that's a debt that can't be ignored.'

'It's no more than anyone might have done, confronted with the circumstances,' said Swann.

'There's those been blessed with charity, no doubt,' agreed Alice. 'While there's some who wouldn't think twice about asking a poor woman home for to put her to Other Purposes,' she added darkly, 'and I mention no names in that connection but I count myself as fortunate to have fallen into *your* hands, sir, and not the hands of another.'

Swann tried to make her listen to reason but Alice could not be persuaded and soon set to work with bucket and brush. She washed the windows and polished the brass but proved too old for heavy duties and sweated herself into such a lather that Swann brought home an Electric Atom suction machine to vacuum the curtains and carpets.

Alice thrived in her new surroundings and now life was torment for Ethel Spooner. She felt threatened by the large intruder and feared she had lost her authority since Alice refused to obey instructions and seemed to take pleasure in stirring up dust.

'Mr Swann said I should never wash the chandeliers,' said Ethel as she watched Alice tempting death by balancing on the arm of a chair and stretching out to the ceiling.

'He's a saint,' puffed Alice. 'But that's no reason to take advantage. Most modern girls is prone to be lazy.'

'I never took advantage,' said Ethel growing tearful and wishing that Alice had never been saved. 'I work all hours to keep this house nice and keep Mr Swann warm and comfortable.'

'You could work all the hours God sends you,' said Alice. 'And you still wouldn't write your name in this filth.'

'It's Mr Swann's orders,' said Ethel. 'I tried to clean out his room but he said he finds it unsettling and he's too old for change and likes to watch the dust grow.'

'I never heard such a story!' hooted Alice.

'It's true!' shouted Ethel.

'I'm not saying you're to blame,' said Alice, 'but, you must admit, you're not very big and the house is too much for an inexperienced slip of a girl to try and manage alone.'

'I'm as strong as a navvy!' protested Ethel, pulling back her shoulders. 'I'm not afraid of hard work.'

And so they engaged in a battle of brooms. They chased each other from room to room, fighting to be first with the polish and the dusters. They bickered over the laundry and squabbled over the cooking. They struggled for the honour of raking the ashes.

This rivalry led to the restoration of formalities not known in the house since the days of Violet Askey. Alice opened a household account book to record the purchase of everything, from a ton of coal to a twist of tea. Daily duties were performed to the chimes of the clock. Guests were no longer shown to the kitchen and, even when he dined alone, Swann was required to take his place at the dining room table.

This state of affairs continued until Alice met with her accident. It was early one Tuesday morning. The house was quiet. Swann had gone to the studio to work on a series of fantasy views involving the Queen of Sheba. Ethel was in the kitchen with a tin of Monkey polish. Alice had found the Electric Atom and managed to haul the machine upstairs ready to vacuum the bedroom carpets.

It might have been a frayed flex or a fault in the primitive engine. No one knew what caused the disaster. The explosion, when it came, set fire to the cleaner and gave Alice such a nasty shock that she fell to the floor in a shower of sparks. Her boot buckles glowed and her petticoats smouldered. Her long hair crackled like kindling.

When Ethel reached the scene she thought Alice had died from spontaneous combustion, overheated and burst into flames. It could happen to anyone. Your vital organs caught alight and melted you inside out. There was no warning. It was like being hit by a thunderbolt.

She looked at the corpse on the carpet, wrapped in a pall of Atomic smoke and she didn't know what to do for the best. So she ran all the way to the studio and dragged Kingdom Swann from his work.

'Alice! Alice!' she shouted. 'Alice is on fire!'

Swann hurried back to Golden Square. When he reached the

scene of the accident the corpse was sitting in a corner of the room, moaning and sucking her fingers. There was nothing left of the vacuum cleaner but a bad smell and a charred box. They opened the window and made Alice comfortable on the bed.

'You're a silly, stubborn, old bodger!' roared Swann as soon as he had surveyed the damage.

'I did it for you, Mr Swann,' whimpered Alice, pulling her fingers from her mouth. 'I wanted to make you happy.' His anger took her by surprise. She didn't deserve a scolding. She felt she had earned some sympathy.

'You nearly killed yourself!' he shouted.

'Yes,' said Alice.

'Is that what you wanted to do for me?'

'No,' said Alice and glared at Ethel who stood there smirking with satisfaction.

'I would rather we were living in filth than we found ourselves fully laundered and dead,' said Swann.

Alice nodded miserably. She hadn't been badly injured but her eyebrows were scorched and her hands so blistered that the doctor was called to wrap them in goose fat and bandages.

For a long time Alice was helpless and Ethel became her nurse. The girl sponged her face and scrubbed her teeth and fed her meals from a spoon. She combed her hair and tied her shoes and buttoned her into her underclothes. Alice complained but, in truth, she enjoyed the attention.

When her hands, at last, healed they had grown so soft and white that, to everyone's great relief, she took care not to callous them again. And, since she no longer placed any trust in mechanical cleaning machines, she seemed content to do nothing.

The dust settled.

'You're a lucky man,' said Cromwell Marsh, 'to be living with a pair of such fine women. If it wasn't for Mrs Marsh, may God keep her hale and hearty, I'd be inclined to envy you Alice.' And his eyes glowed unusually bright.

'I'm living content,' admitted Swann. 'I've no cause for complaint.'

He was wrong.

28

He was sitting in the drawing room one evening, digesting a slice of veal and ham pie, when he noticed a strange clot of darkness trapped beneath a *bonheur-du-jour*. He lowered the newspaper from his face and stared at this murky ectoplasm and, as he watched, he thought it moved. It must be a trick of the light. He was going mad. He was going blind. His eyes had been hurt by the years of burning magnesium wire. He left his chair and crept towards the apparition and, as he approached, it seemed to change shape, grow arms and legs and a set of large, brown eyes.

Swann sprang back in alarm. It was an idiot-faced boy, no more than six years old, dressed in a woman's cotton chemise. They stared at each other in silence, both bewildered by the encounter. The old man pulled on his beard like a bell rope. The child took comfort by sucking its thumb.

Once Swann had recovered from the shock of this sullen intruder, and was satisfied that it wasn't likely to scratch or bite, he began to feel that perhaps it should give him an explanation. Who was it, by thunder, and by what odd sequence of events did it find itself in his room? He opened his mouth and shut it again. He didn't know how to address a child.

He tried a smile, half-closed his eyes and bared his teeth, but it made not the slightest impression. The child sat, chewing its thumb and blinking at Swann with large, suspicious eyes. Finally he rang for Ethel.

'Please sir, with your permission, this one here is Billy,' said Ethel, looking very flustered as she hurried into the room. She fished the child from its hiding place and lifted it into her arms. 'I had to bring him along, sir, since the old one can't care for him proper. He'll be no trouble and I've got him sleeping with me and Alice until his chest is stronger.'

'What's wrong with his chest?' enquired Swann, finding the courage to poke at the child with his finger.

'He suffers from the damp, sir,' said Ethel. She pulled the chemise around the child's throat and gently chucked his chin.

'And what happened to his clothes?' said Swann. He accepted the creature now as one of the clothes-peg family, although with its hair combed down and the crust of filth gone from its face, it was changed beyond recognition.

'Begging your pardon, sir, his clothes fell to bits when we washed him so Alice lent him a vest.'

At that moment the child pulled the thumb from its mouth, cocked its face flirtatiously at Swann and gave the most enchanting smile.

'Poor little bugger!' grinned Kingdom Swann. 'Why, he looks so small he must be half-starved.'

'Oh, he don't eat much,' said Ethel quickly. 'He's not used to food – so he'll be no trouble on that account. Can I have him stay, sir, until his chest is mended?'

'You keep him here and fatten him,' said Swann, 'and tomorrow, you must buy him a suit of clothes.'

Ethel was so happy that she burst into tears and spirited the child away for a cup of something in the kitchen.

Swann settled back in his chair. He didn't know what to make of it. He didn't like the idea of having children loose in the house, he was far too old to learn to like them, but the boy was here and couldn't be sent back into the slums. Swann remembered the journey he had made with Ethel, the stinking maze of murderous alleys, the smell in that dreadful, crowded room. He supposed a small boy would present no trouble. As far as he could determine, the average boy had a talent for nothing much more than farting, scratching and picking the nose. But how did you look after one? Ask a woman. Leave the affair to Ethel and Alice.

It was several days before he told Cromwell Marsh about the unlikely visitor. 'He's an ugly little squab,' said Swann. 'I can't say I care for the look of him.'

'A child can't be judged by no physiognomy,' laughed Marsh, amused by the old man's predicament. He thought it would do him the power of good to have a child about the house. 'I've known some horrible crawlers grow into splendid, big women. Besides, no matter how queer or demented they looks, you soon grows very fond of 'em.'

'But when do they learn to talk?' complained Swann. 'This one must be six years old and doesn't so much as blow a bubble.'

'Well, that must depend on the size of the infant's brain and the kinds of food you gives it,' said Marsh. 'It's how you stuffs 'em makes all the difference. Mrs Marsh was most pernickety on the question of wholesome and healthy meals and we was blessed with seven children, if you count the three we lost to the pox.'

'And what do you suggest?'

'Plenty of white meat. Boiled chicken. Rabbit. Tripe and onions. Calf's foot jelly,' said Marsh, ticking them off on his fingers.

'I'll tell Alice to place an order with the butcher.'

'I don't suppose you know the whereabouts of the father?' said Marsh, after a while.

'I never heard speak of one,' said Swann.

'And the mother?'

'Now there's a curiosity,' said Swann. 'The one they call their mother looks too old to bear infants.'

'Is that right?' said Marsh thoughtfully.

'She's a bundle of rag and bones.'

'Well, children, in my experience, don't grow from seed potatoes,' said Cromwell Marsh with a grin.

'Nothing would surprise me,' said Swann.

In the weeks that followed Billy's arrival Ethel and Alice did everything they could to prevent the child from crossing their master's path. He was kept shut away in the kitchen and yet, whenever he managed to escape, Swann seemed delighted to see him. The child was baffled by all the attention but quickly learned that the old man's pockets were loaded with packets of aniseed balls.

And then, one night, there were two of them. The second was even smaller and more downcast than the original. It had ginger hair and a squint. Billy led him to the big man's pockets where they both fished in silence for aniseed.

'This one here is Wilfred, sir, who we had to bring to stay since he pines so hard for his brother, Billy,' explained Ethel, when called upon for assistance.

'Where will you keep him?' said Swann, peering down at the child. Wilfred grew bashful and squirmed and pretended to study his feet.

'He'll sleep with me and Alice, sir,' she said hopefully. 'There's plenty of room if we squeeze together.'

Swann frowned. 'It doesn't sound entirely decent,' he said. 'It doesn't seem altogether hygienic.'

'We'll wash him regular, sir, and make sure he don't wet the sheets,' said Ethel anxiously, pulling Wilfred towards her legs and wrapping his head in her skirt. The child gave a yelp and the aniseed ball fell out of its mouth. The sugar pill rolled across the carpet gathering crumbs and dust.

'No,' said Swann firmly, shaking his head. 'It's time we took up another bed that's a suitable size for infants.'

Ethel felt so relieved she threw her arms around Kingdom Swann and pushed a kiss through his beard.

Swann soon accepted Wilfred as easily as he'd taken to Billy and ordered new clothes and a greater supply of calf's foot jelly.

A month later there were three of them. The two small boys had been joined by a girl no more than four years old. Her name was Grace. She was found in the dining room, sitting behind a scuttle of coals. Her arms and legs were covered in sores and most of her teeth were missing. She looked very similar to her mother.

'She ain't catching,' said Ethel, 'and she's ever so good-hearted. It seemed too cruel to keep her away from her little brothers since they've always been so attached.'

'But she needs attention,' protested Swann, as he looked at the rash of sores. 'This poor child needs a doctor.'

He would have said more but Ethel had gone. She ran for her

coat and hat and in less than half an hour a doctor had been summoned to examine the child. He painted the sores with disinfectant, prescribed fresh greens and regular fruit and told Swann to put the patient to bed. She couldn't sleep with the others so they gave her a room of her own in the attic.

By the end of the summer there were four children in the house. The fourth was called George and came to stay because he was missing his sister.

'She was like a mother to him, sir, and he won't touch his food since she's been missing.'

He was a sad little creature with a mournful face and a nose as bent as a cashew nut. He was wearing a secondhand birthday frock and had a ribbon in his hair.

'What's the time, mister?' he said, when Swann bent down to admire his frock.

'He talks!' said Swann drawing back in astonishment.

'Well, he does and he doesn't, sir,' said Ethel, rather perplexed. 'I *suppose* he talks, in a manner of speaking, but them are the only words he learned.'

'What's the time, mister?' said George.

Swann found he couldn't resist him.

Ethel and Alice scrubbed the children and dressed them and kept them as neat as dolls. But they were a strange crowd with their lopsided faces and stunted limbs. They clustered in corners, shocking and silent, staring at Swann in fascination, while he for his part took to looking through cupboards and boxes, searching for others from the tribe who might yet be waiting, undiscovered.

29

The last child home was little Bertie. He was three years old and blessed with a face like a small bull-terrier. He arrived one night, howling with cold and wrapped in the arms of the mother. Alice let the old woman into the kitchen and sat her down to warm in front of the Livingstone range. She had been evicted from her room in Heaven's Yard since, without her team of peg-doll makers, she couldn't afford to pay the rent. It was no surprise to Swann.

They gave her the room with the Chinese curtains, which she took without a word of protest and, once she'd been washed and fitted with one of Ethel's clean frocks, they led her back to the kitchen for a hot plate of kidney and bacon.

It was then that Swann discovered she was far less decrepit than he had supposed and might have passed for handsome had she but owned a set of teeth. She was a small woman in her late forties with a hollow face and shrunken jaws. It was only her mouth, her wild hair and the noises she made as she sucked at her food, that made her seem so demented.

For the first few days she did nothing but lie in her bed, groaning and grinding her gums, hoping to win Swann's sympathy by feigning a close acquaintance with death. But then, since no one threatened her, she soon found her health completely restored and spent all her time in a kitchen chair, taking tea and biscuits with Alice.

The family flourished in its new home and Swann learned to live with the infestation of children. It was a big house and he tried to keep to his own private quarters. But he found there were children everywhere. They piddled in his Sunday best boots, puked on his carpets and picked the paper from the walls. They trapped themselves in his wardrobe and crawled beneath his bed. They wedged themselves up chimneys and ate the coals in the grates.

When these things happened he called for Alice who scolded Ethel who tried to keep order by banging skulls with a clothes brush.

'They don't have enough to occupy 'em,' Alice warned him. 'They need a regular thrashing. A leather slipper night and morning.'

'It sounds rather harsh,' said Swann.

'They appreciate the security when you give it to 'em regular,' said Alice.

'Why aren't they at their lessons?' said Swann.

'Lessons?' said Alice, looking alarmed.

'Reading, writing and arithmetic,' chanted Swann. 'Geography, history and music. Poetry, painting and literature. Latin and Greek. Education. Lessons for life.'

Alice frowned and shook her head. 'I don't know much about learning,' she said suspiciously. 'I keep the account books nice and neat and that's enough for me. I never had no complaints. And I never met a butcher yet who spoke to me in Latin. If you want to know about education I think you'll have to ask Ethel.'

'They can't be allowed to grow up wild,' grumbled Swann, 'or we'll find them into all kinds of mischief.'

'I'm sure I do my best to keep them from under your feet,' said Alice, looking wounded.

'I caught Wilfred eating a bag of buttons,' said Swann gravely. 'And when I tried to open his mouth the little bugger bit me.'

'A good thrashing night and morning. That's my prescription,' said Alice stubbornly. 'You can't have a better lesson for life.'

Swann now felt responsible for his newly adopted family. It was a burden at his time of life. It wasn't enough, as he'd fondly supposed, merely to feed and clothe them. He'd been given the task of taming them. He must educate this barbarous tribe and lend it some sense of purpose. He could organise drawing lessons and tutor them in the rudiments of anatomy and perspective. But he lacked the patience or skill to teach them to read and write.

After brooding on this problem for several days he decided he should recruit a properly qualified governess. An energetic, modern girl with a general knowledge of the arts. If he couldn't drive the children to school then the school would be brought to them.

And then, one evening, Swann came home to the smell of paint and hot fish glue. When he followed his nose he found the Spooners at the scullery table, putting together clothes-peg dolls.

'What's happening here?' he roared.

'They're making their dolls, sir,' said Ethel, looking startled as he thundered into the room. She must have forgotten the time and his supper wasn't ready.

'What dolls?' demanded Swann, charging forward and snagging a clothes-line with his head. 'Dolls? What are they planning to do with dolls?'

'Little George goes out to sell them,' said Alice. 'He shows a natural gift for it.'

'You send him out on the street?' shouted Swann, trying to pull himself free from the line and trampling a basket of clothes-pegs. 'A child of mine sent out walking the streets!' He had rescued these people from poverty and now, here they were in his scullery, rebuilding the room they had shared in the back of Heaven's Yard!

'Oh, yes, sir,' said Ethel proudly.

'We send him out along Regent Street,' said Alice, 'when the weather permits and he comes home by way of Bond Street. When the weather is nasty he goes down as far as Oxford Street and shelters under Selfridges.'

'Folks can't resist him,' said Ethel.

'They think he's simple,' said Alice.

'He is simple,' said Ethel.

'But it don't stop him counting his coppers,' said Alice.

George glanced up at Kingdom Swann and wiped his nose

on his hand. 'What's the time, mister?' He grinned hopefully and waggled his scissors in the air.

'But they don't have to slave for coppers!' shouted Swann, turning his rage on Ethel. 'Good God, don't I provide for them?'

'Yes, sir,' said Ethel, dropping a curtsey.

'Don't I dress them and feed them and keep them warm?'

'Yes, sir,' said Ethel, dropping a curtsey and this time falling down in a heap and pulling her apron over her face.

'Damn!' shouted Swann. He had grown so red in the face and was blowing so much steam that the children now jumped from the table and ran to comfort him, clutching at his arms and legs and pulling on his sleeves. Ethel trembled on the brink of tears.

'It's a force of habit, sir,' said Alice. 'Old Mrs Spooner says she wants to pay for her lodgings.'

'You're a lovely, lovely gent, Mr Swann, a very lovely gent!' shouted old Mrs Spooner, smacking her gums. 'And here's me lodgings for the week,' she added confidentially, as she pressed a shilling into his hand.

'But you shouldn't have to make them work,' said Swann, trying, in vain, to return the coin. 'You could be sending them out to school. Don't you want them to have a proper education?'

Old Mrs Spooner looked shocked. 'I don't believe in it, sir. There's too much reading and writing in life. And once they've learned you how, why, you just can't stop yourself doing it. But does it make a man happy? Does it make a man healthy and wise? No, sir! I've known educated men. Wilfred's father was an educated man…'

'And they *hanged* him,' said Alice.

'You're a lovely gent, Mr Swann, but I wouldn't want no reading and writing to break an infant's heart.'

'But Ethel can read and write,' argued Swann, pulling in fury at his beard. His dream of recruiting a governess was rapidly evaporating.

'She gets that from Gloria and she's full of the airs and graces,' snorted Mrs Spooner indignantly.

'I never meant no harm!' honked Ethel, blowing her nose. 'I wanted to take them from under your feet!' And she burst, at last, into floods of tears.

'You can't stop 'em working their trade,' shouted Alice, folding Ethel into her arms. 'They was born to it, Mr Swann.'

Swann shook his head. 'Damn!' He turned around and, with Grace clinging to one leg and Wilfred biting the other, waded from the room.

30

He had become a factory owner. He was mortified. Every morning before he left for the studio he would creep downstairs and peek through the scullery door as if he were stealing a view through a peepshow machine. The children worked from dawn until dusk, cutting and sticking the paper skirts, while the mother pecked at the pegs with her paint brush. Two dots and a dash. Two dots and a dash.

He bought the children expensive toys and made a nursery in the attic, purchased a set of tiny armchairs and painted the walls with jungle scenes, teeming with panthers and parrots. He found a rocking horse and a phonograph and a set of improving picture books. He collected jigsaw puzzles and a long line of clockwork novelties including a mouse with a tambourine and a pig that played the trumpet. When he had finished he made them sit in the little armchairs and tried to teach them how to be children. He crawled around on his hands and knees making farmyard noises and laughing at the mouse with the tambourine. But they treated his efforts with suspicion. They slept in the nursery, too tired for games, curled into balls like a litter of puppies. They lived and worked in the scullery.

When his plan to save the children failed he turned his attention to old Mrs Spooner and tried to ruin her with drink. Finding she had a taste for beer he stacked crates of stout beneath the table, hoping to soften her brain and spoil her aim with the paintbrush. But the mother could drink like a sailor, thrived on her rations and only seemed to work faster.

Finally, as if he wanted to shame them or perhaps because he could not believe the evidence of his own eyes, he took down a camera and photographed them. This created a small commotion and work was suspended for a few minutes while old Mrs

Spooner combed everyone's hair and took care to hide her own grey shock inside a large poke-bonnet.

There was no artistry in these pictures. He framed his subjects as he found them, hunched at the table, stupid and staring, with the clothes-lines hanging above their heads like so much festival bunting. He spent a long time pretending to fiddle with the camera, making all sorts of small adjustments, not for any practical reason but purely for the pleasure he took in keeping the workforce sitting idle. And when he was finished he hurried off to the studio and ordered Marsh to develop the plates.

'Look at 'em!' he growled as the prints were set out to dry. 'You'd think they were living in slavery!'

'It don't look so bad,' said Cromwell Marsh.

'It's the most degrading sight I've put before the camera!' roared Swann. 'Crazy people! Wasted lives!'

'It could be worse,' said Marsh. 'You keep the scullery nice and warm.'

'But look at 'em!' shrieked Swann. 'Look at 'em!'

Old mother Spooner, in her big poke-bonnet, looked like a pantomime dame. The children, caught by a trick of the light, had the tragic air of emaciated gnomes.

'It's not a pretty sight,' grinned Marsh and, in a moment of mischief, submitted one of the prints to the New Photographic Club's London Art Treasure Exhibition.

31

The Peg-Doll Workshop was awarded a silver medal and the *Journal of Modern Photography* (September 1912) carried a column of fulsome praise for the largely unknown photographer.

Swann was most alarmed by the news. 'You shouldn't have done it,' he roared, dragging Marsh from the darkroom. 'You shouldn't have done it without my permission.'

'Where's the harm?' blinked Marsh.

'What if they want to see more of my work? What are we going to show them?' He had spent all his time in pursuit of cavorting, full-blown nudes and his single public success was a picture of half-witted infants!

'We'll think of something,' said Cromwell Marsh. Thieves and cut-throats. Cripples and beggars. *London Low Life* by Kingdom Swann. He was full of ideas when he sensed there was money to be made.

'Don't involve me in your hare-brained schemes,' said Swann, in a fright. 'I'll have nothing to do with it.' He waved Marsh away and fled up the steps of the wooden stage.

Marsh shrugged. 'You won a medal and a mention in the *Journal,*' he said, still feeling rather pleased with himself.

'Damn nonsense,' said Swann.

'Have you seen it?' said Marsh, pulling the magazine from his pocket.

Swann shook his head.

'Shall I read it to you?'

Swan grunted and sat down on a roll of canvas clouds. 'Among the gum-prints, smudge prints, splodges, dodges and plain buffoonery that we have come to expect from the New Photographic Club's exhibitions, we are pleased to find a welcome return to the grand European traditions of photographic realism. In *The Peg-Doll Workshop* by Kingdom Swann Esq we witness a triumph of naturalism, both in content and treatment, to rival the great Oscar Gustav Rejlander...'

'Rejlander!' exploded Kingdom Swann. 'There was nothing natural in that old fraud. The man was so sweet he farted violets.'

'I suppose they mean by natural them pictures he took of little orphans acting wistful,' said Cromwell Marsh. 'He used to be famous for 'em.'

'They couldn't stop him!' shouted Swann. 'If he found an urchin in the street he'd have it into the studio with a halo on its head before it had time to shout for help!'

'Shall I finish?' said Marsh, shaking the journal.

'Is there more?'

'Yes.'

'Read it!' stormed Swann.

' ...to rival the great Oscar Gustav Rejlander. Everything about this prize exhibit is simple and unpretentious; the light bold, the composition dynamic and the artist's sympathy for the plight of his miserable subject shines through with an absolute clarity. In these days of myopic illusionism we can only congratulate Mr Swann on his fortitude in fighting the decadence and presenting such frank views of everyday life.'

'Is that it?' said Swann.

'That's it,' said Marsh, carefully folding the magazine and pushing it into his pocket.

Swann was silent for a long time. 'I've spent twenty years taking frank views of life,' he said at last, staring down on the studio. 'The nudes are frank. Life's no franker than Gloria Spooner when the wind is up her skirt.'

'If we sent her out on exhibition we'd both be arrested tomorrow,' said Marsh. It made him sad. It was such a waste.

Swann sighed and scratched his beard. 'They made it a crime to take photographs of a woman's article of joy, but show her toiling, dirty and wretched and they call you an artist and give you a medal.'

'Photography beautifies everything,' said Marsh. 'That's the curse of the camera.'

'My solitary public triumph: the view of a London scullery,' muttered Swann. He prised back the lid of the costume trunk and plunged his arms into underwear.

'It's an odd world and no mistake,' said Marsh. 'These days it's all views of working life. And the more degraded the work the better they seem to like it.'

'What does it do for them?' said Swann. 'What? Does it satisfy some terrible, morbid appetite? It's disgusting. It gives me the shivers. Why do they want to see it?'

'I'm buggered if I know,' said Cromwell Marsh. 'Poverty and suffering is thought to be very picturesque.'

'There's enough misery in the world without hanging it on the walls,' said Swann, as he fondled a silk chemise. 'You can't cure human misery by framing it up and calling it art.'

'I suppose they believe they're pioneers uncovering hidden aspects of life. There can't be an animal, bird or flower that hasn't been made a picture postcard. You can buy a view of Abyssinia as easy as buying a bag of sultanas. Kings and queens can be bought by the dozen. Nearly everything in the world has been photographed. Everything. They'll soon be going to the slaughter house and the lunatic asylum.'

'Nonsense!' said Swann.

'There's nothing too strong that can't now be brought to public attention by way of the photograph,' warned Marsh.

'Except men and women engaged in the simple pleasures of love,' growled Swann.

'True,' said Marsh. 'But everything else is thought suitable for intimate investigation. There's a photographer in Bristol who takes his camera to hospital.'

'There's nothing to see in a hospital but rows of old men wearing new pyjamas. There's nothing on view but their suffering.'

'That's the attraction,' said Cromwell Marsh. 'He recently attended a serious amputation.'

Swann was flabbergasted. He pressed the chemise against

his mouth. 'You mean, I can show a man,' he said, 'crouched upon a naked woman if he's strictly employed to hack off her legs!'

'Well, I don't know,' frowned Marsh. 'I suppose she would still be required to maintain a degree of modesty.'

'And they call that art?' bellowed Swann.

Marsh gave out a hollow laugh and went back to work in the dark-room. 'These days you can't blow your nose without *some-one* calling it art.'

The medal, received by Cromwell Marsh on behalf of the aged photographer, was a milled silver piece about the size of a Huntley & Palmer biscuit. It had been embossed with the profile of Louis-Jacques-Mande Daguerre and the simple inscription: VENI VIDI VICI. Swann had it pierced for an albert and hung it from his waistcoat pocket.

32

The award was followed by a period of doubt and confusion for Swann. He began to plan larger and more elaborate assemblies of nudes, defying the fashion for views of the humdrum and commonplace. He bought rolls of cartography paper and spent hours at the table, sketching historical melodramas of breathtaking size and pomposity.

Marsh knew, at a glance, that these extravagant battles and banquets could never be turned into photographs. *A Slave Girl Offered to Hannibal on the Shield of a Roman General* required thirty dancers, a battlefield and an elephant in armour. *Alexander Conquers the Punjab* needed a dozen horses and a war machine that was large enough to knock a hole in a castle. But when he tried to persuade the old man to exercise moderation Swann grew frustrated and angry. Retreating from the modern world, where an empty chair was thought picturesque enough to be posed in front of the camera, he'd committed himself to a grand Swann-song in the cause of heroic photography.

After several arguments with Marsh on the cost of horses and elephants, Swann withdrew his most ambitious proposals and settled, instead, on *Vandals at the Persian Gates.* An old-fashioned struggle of good and evil to feature a dozen bearded giants, a harem of nudes, a brace of Nubian guards and a leopard.

'Where will I find a leopard?' cried Marsh.

'I don't know!' shouted Swann. 'Where's your imagination? I offer you my genius and all you can see are problems.'

Marsh complained bitterly that even if they found the beast they wouldn't find twelve giants and if they found twelve giants they would never find the Nubians and if they found the Nubians they would never fit such a troupe on the stage.

'Find me a bigger stage!' roared Swann. 'Find me an old theatre with wings and drops and all the trimmings. We'll assemble a living painting. The biggest picture in the whole damn history of classical photography. Nudes of all nations heaped in human pyramids. Furies in the footlights. Angels in the flies.'

'Impossible!' said Marsh, flapping up and down in despair. 'You can't let Vandals loose raping women, bold as brass, on the London stage. We'll all be arrested for God-knows-what! You might as well put 'em out on a barge and sail 'em naked along the Thames!'

'Cleopatra!' shouted Swann, his eyes ablaze with inspiration.

'No,' pleaded Marsh.

'Yes!' raved Swann. *'Cleopatra Carried Aboard Her Funeral Barge*. Trumpeters and peacocks. Slave-girls and blackamoors!' His eyes bulged. His beard was flecked with foam.

'It's not practical,' moaned Marsh, who was now so agitated he looked ready to burst into tears.

'It would be a revolution!' cried Swann. 'Unwrapping God's most lovely creation in the midst of the natural landscape. We'll do away with canvas clouds and plaster of Paris pillars. We'll take to the rivers and meadows of England, work in the glorious light of the sun.'

'Revolution?' echoed Marsh. 'We'd most likely cause a full-blown riot trying to follow your plan.'

'What's wrong?' shouted Swann impatiently.

'We'd have every tinker and tailor in London straining for a view,' said Marsh. 'That's what's wrong! Imagine the disturbance. Think of the excitement. They'd bring along a barrel organ. They'd be selling nuts and oranges. We'd cause such a riot they'd call out the army, I shouldn't be surprised.'

'We don't want spectators,' said Swann.

'Naked women on parade in the middle of the public highway? There's no avoiding it,' said Marsh.

'We'll choose a sheltered part of the river and work behind a tarpaulin screen,' said Swann.

'We can't work in a circus tent!' said the horrified Marsh, beginning to wonder if this were a dream or some peculiar sort of joke. 'We'd draw the riff-raff from miles around. You'd turn us into a side-show attraction.'

But Swann had stopped listening. He seemed determined to show his talent the light of day. It was perfect. The barge brimming over with funeral flowers. The water sucking at the blackamoors' feet. Cleopatra borne aloft by slaves. The wind at her hair. The sun behind her head like a beaten copper plate.

'I'll leave you to make the arrangements,' he said.

So Marsh was sent out to search the Thames for a stately Nile barge. He ventured as far as Stepney before he found a suitable hulk. It was moored at a wharf not far from Limehouse Reach. The owner was puzzled when Marsh expressed an interest since the vessel was old and rusted away and she barely had enough wind in her belly to keep herself afloat. But Marsh was so determined and the owner so pleased to be rid of her that a bargain was struck and arrangements made to tow the barge to a more secluded landing stage.

As soon as Swann had inspected the craft, and declared her fit for his purpose, they set about her transformation. Carpenters were called to build a raised deck and disguise the worst of the decay with suitable portions of timber. Artists were commissioned to paint her flanks in designs that were generally thought to be most fitting for Pharaohs. Swann provided the working drawings of sacred birds and magic symbols. He selected the colours for his designs and issued written instructions on their mixing and application.

But the work proved costly and difficult. The carpenters cheated them. The artists were lazy and wasted the paint, fell from their slings in a drunken stupor and had to be saved from drowning. The barge broke loose from her moorings and drifted as far as Greenwich, creating havoc along the way and nearly sinking a paddle-steamer, before they caught her and dragged her home. She sprang her bilge and was patched and the patch sprang a leak and she had to be patched again.

Marsh begged the old man to forget his flight of fancy for

fear it would bankrupt the studio. But Swann remained in a confident mood. His dream was taking shape. He was already trying to order the peacocks and searching for Cleopatra. It wasn't until the barge fell apart in a storm, and disappeared through the stinking mud, that he lost heart, at last, in the enterprise. Then he withdrew, defeated, and spent all his time in the studio, arguing angrily with himself and walking the empty stage.

33

It was at this time that Swann accepted his last, and most notorious, commission. *The Portrait of Rupert Gladstone's Mistress.*

Gladstone was a man of wealth and influence. He was a scholar and collector of antique porcelain. He lived, alone, in a mansion near Hampstead Heath and, despite all the comforts money could buy, was subject to fits of melancholy. When such a mood overtook him he could neither eat nor sleep, found sunlight unendurable and shut himself away in the cellars. The cause of his affliction had never been discovered and many cures had been tried and abandoned.

His faithful friends were always searching for new ways to lift his spirits and so, one day, when he asked them about a photographer to glorify a mistress they were anxious to satisfy the whim. They were surprised by the odd request since Gladstone had shown no interest in women, but all were agreed that the man to approach was the venerable Kingdom Swann.

Swann was apathetic to the idea but Cromwell Marsh persuaded him that Gladstone was worthy of their attention.

'He's very high-falutin in the art and museum world. A proper old-fashioned connoisseur.'

'And the woman?' said Swann.

'Now that's the interesting part,' said Marsh, winking and tapping his nose. 'Nobody knows her name. But it's rumoured she comes from an ancient royal family.'

'She'll be one of the servants,' sighed Swann. 'Whenever there's a mystery woman it's usually one of the servants. A maid arrived from the country or a high-buttoned governess.' He smiled as he sucked at his whiskers.

'Remember Sir Bentley Fowler? He brought along his

governess. He wanted her portrayed as a Roman gladiator. She already owned the costume and we supplied a chainnet and trident. Big woman. Strong as an Indian buffalo. He liked her to lift him up and carry him around.'

'Servant? I doubts it,' said Marsh. 'He keeps a very limited staff and all of 'em are men. He don't like women about the house. He finds their manner disturbing.' Marsh, as usual, seemed to know more than was good for him.

Swann was curious enough to accept the commission and Rupert Gladstone arrived in Piccadilly on the following Sunday morning. He was a tall, pale, middle-aged man, dressed for a wedding and smelling strongly of lavender. His grey hair had been oiled flat and his collar starched to a cutting edge. He removed one glove, solemnly shook Kingdom Swann by the hand and stared around the studio.

'Has she not yet arrived?' he enquired, frowning, fumbling for his pocket watch. He looked worried, as if he regretted everything and might yet cancel the appointment.

'Begging your pardon,' said Cromwell Marsh, 'but it's usual, under the circumstance, for a gent to arrive with the lady in question, safely secured on his arm. It helps prevent any misunderstanding.'

'No,' said Gladstone distractedly. 'No. She's more than I can manage alone. Travel, you know, is such a burden.'

Marsh looked at Swann and Swann looked surprised and Marsh turned back to their visitor. 'Perhaps you'd care for a small glass of something to settle the nerves while you're waiting?' he suggested.

At that moment there was a noise at the front of the shop, a scuffling and the sound of men cursing. Gladstone rushed out and returned, a few moments later, with two men bearing a small wooden coffin. He made them lay the box upon the stage, paid them, handsomely, and led them back to the street with instructions to return in one hour. Marsh saw them climb aboard a motor wagon as he went out to lock the shop.

When all this had been accomplished Gladstone took a key from his purse and gently opened the coffin.

'Maria,' he whispered. 'Maria.'

He gazed inside, his face aquiver with great excitement and his eyes beginning to fill with tears. Slowly, and with extraordinary tenderness, he reached down and pulled a woman into his arms. She was a tiny, dark-haired creature, not more than a child, wrapped in the rags of a wedding dress. As they watched, he lifted the woman free from the casket and placed her down at his feet.

'Oh, my God, she's dead!' groaned Marsh, tottering backwards across the stage.

'No, sir!' hissed Gladstone, grabbing Marsh by the scruff of the neck and shaking him rigid with fright. 'No, sir, not dead but sleeping…'

Marsh knelt down to look at the corpse and on closer inspection found it was worse than he'd first imagined. Her face was a ghastly varnished mask, the skin shrunk tight against the skull, the eyes wide open and hard as glass, the jaw loose and the teeth exposed. The wretched girl had been stuffed! He was looking at the work of some diabolical taxidermist!

Her name was Maria Castellana, a gypsy girl from Seville. Rupert Gladstone had met her in Paris and, falling hopelessly in love, had followed her over the mountains to Spain. At first she had fled from his embrace but gradually he had won her heart and a marriage was arranged.

There were many obstacles on the path to their future happiness. She could not speak a word of English and he could not master Spanish. He was forced to fight a duel with her brother (for reasons of honour so obscure he never made any sense of them) and, afraid of offending the family by butchering one of its favourite sons, allowed himself to be badly wounded. He spent several months in the gypsy camp recovering from these injuries. Meanwhile the family grew suspicious of the pale, young foreigner and demanded he pay an exorbitant dowry before he could claim the girl as his bride. He had to send home for the money and have the banknotes converted to gold. And then, on the eve of the wedding, Maria fell sick with the fever and died.

Rupert Gladstone returned to London and wasted away with grief. He shut himself into the house and lived in a state of perpetual mourning. He thought he would never see her again.

But the gypsies were people of honour and since Rupert Gladstone had paid for the girl they promised themselves he should not be cheated. So they skinned her and boned her and pickled her pelt like a sheet of fine and expensive leather. The skeleton was stuffed with horsehair and a seamstress employed to stitch back the skin. Seven months and three days later Maria Castellana was delivered to the Hampstead house, rouged, powdered, dressed for the wedding and securely packed in an olive-wood box.

Gladstone was overwhelmed with joy to have his love returned to him. His sleeping beauty. His enchanted gypsy princess. He built her a boudoir in the cellars and equipped it with every comfort. He took down silk carpets and a feather bed and spent every evening, locked away, singing to her while he brushed her hair.

His friends, knowing nothing of the secret, were startled by his changed appearance whenever he emerged from the cellar. A few days locked beneath the ground never failed to restore his health. He would be seized by fits of giggling and sudden outbursts of violent laughter. He was light. He was gay. In short, he was raving mad.

Now he stood on Swann's stage, with the hideous creature slumped at his feet, trying to wrench the wedding dress over her leathery shoulders. She gasped and creaked at the seams, her breasts caught up in the rotting silk like darkly polished plums.

Swann tried everything he knew to make him return the corpse to its coffin. She wasn't a suitable studio subject and, besides, what purpose would it serve to hoist her before the camera? Her master was free to play with her and marvel at her private parts whenever he desired. She wasn't likely to run away or desert him for another lover. Why did he want her photographed?

'Mice!' hissed Gladstone fearfully, hooking his hand

beneath the girl's chin. Her belly jerked forward, as tight as a gourd, and where it was sewn between her legs erupted a long, ragged horsehair beard. The mice were building a nest in her notch. The Spanish love-doll was in serious danger of falling apart.

This new information, far from gaining Swann's sympathy, only served to heighten his horror. He shook his head and scampered towards the door.

'Stand your ground!' ordered Rupert Gladstone.

'No!' wheezed Swann. 'No, I can't do it! You've stolen the unhappy girl from the grave. She's dead, God help us, the girl is dead!'

'Not dead but sleeping!' raved Gladstone.

'Give her a Christian burial and let her sleep in peace!' shouted Swann from the far side of the studio.

'Don't be a fool!' screamed Gladstone, running to the edge of the stage. Maria Castellana creaked and flopped forward, wedging her face between her knees. 'Stop or I'll use my revolver!'

Marsh gave a shout and fell to the floor. 'Mercy! Don't shoot!' he pleaded, wrapping his head in his arms.

Swann turned around to confront the stage. Gladstone had pulled a gun from his coat and pushed the barrel into his ear. He laughed wildly. His finger trembled against the trigger. He threatened to blow out his brains.

Kingdom Swann took the photograph.

34

He never accepted another commission. For more than ten years he had photographed the mistresses of London's high society. They had been presented to him in all of nature's variety and never once had he failed to make them feel beautiful. But Maria Castellana had defeated him, had mocked him with her sepulchral smile and stubborn horsehair body.

When requests were made by General Cotton for private studies of his latest conquest, a ripe and red-haired girl he had pillaged on a raid of Weymouth, Marsh was obliged to refuse him. He hinted that Swann was engaged in more urgent and challenging work. But, in truth, Kingdom Swann did nothing.

Marsh tried setting him off on two sets of novelty pictures using the best of Mrs Beeton's academy. *Ragtime Raptures, or The Dancing Lesson* and *When Amazons Mount their Bicycles*. But Swann found no excitement in them. The old man had lost his enthusiasm.

The following year the suffragettes began a campaign of terror. A bomb was found attached to the railings of the Bank of England and another inside St Paul's Cathedral. Millions of women marched through London, shouting slogans and banging drums. They threw stones at windows and tried to set fire to the Royal Academy.

'It's the same thing every year,' said Marsh cheerfully. 'It just wouldn't be summer without a women's march.'

'They'll kill someone before they've finished,' said Swann.

A few days later a woman threw herself beneath the King's horse at the Derby and was trampled to death. A man tried to follow her example during the Gold Cup at Ascot but survived, disgraced, and was quickly forgotten.

'Why don't the government give 'em the vote?' said Swann.

'They don't have the brains for that sort of business,' said Marsh. 'They're like children. You can't expect them to think for themselves. They have to be told what's good for them. And, besides, the vote won't be the end of it,' he added darkly. 'The next thing you know we'll have a petticoat parliament and then we'll have serious trouble.'

'Nonsense!' said Swann. 'They just say that to frighten you.'

'You wait,' said Marsh. 'It's the future. As soon as women get the vote we'll have all manner of mischief.'

'It makes no difference either way,' said Swann. 'A man still won't be able to find honest work. His children will still be going hungry. There'll be just as much misery in the world.'

'There's never no work for an honest man because there's always a woman,' said Marsh, 'prepared to work for half the wages.'

'I'll never understand why women *want* to work. There's nothing noble in wasting your days pushing paper in some pokey office or risking your life in a factory, chopping your fingers through a sausage machine. There's nothing noble in reducing yourself to drudgery and selling your life by the hour. You'd think they'd be happy to stay at home with their sewing and their watercolours. It's the privilege awarded them.'

'It's the choice they're demanding,' said Cromwell Marsh. 'The privilege to pick and choose.'

'The poor don't have that privilege!' shouted Swann. 'They have always been forced to work and in the filthiest conditions!'

'Oh, it's not the dirty work they want,' said Marsh. 'These women want to be chemists and bishops.'

'Chemists and bishops!' roared Kingdom Swann. 'Is it nothing but a parlour game?'

'It might sound like fun and games to the greatly superior masculine brain but there's women in prison starving to death for the sake of such curious notions.'

'If they must leave home and hearth,' said Swann, 'let them, by their good example, bring some light and hope to the world. Don't let them squander their lives like the men.'

'And what would you suggest, Mr Swann?'

The old photographer puffed out his chest and slipped his hands behind his beard. 'The world needs sculptors and painters,' he said. 'The world needs music and poetry. We've seen enough factories and sweat-shops. Imagine a land where every woman was taught to be an accomplished artist. Think of the civilisation we'd build!'

'But if women was artists,' smirked Marsh, 'who would we have to be models?'

'The men,' said Swann, surprised by such a foolish question. 'Men by their own brute strength transformed into graceful gods.'

'I never saw much evidence in the case of Lanky Parsons!' laughed Marsh.

'You'd have to view him through a woman's eyes,' said Swann.

'You always was a thinker,' chortled Marsh, very much amused. 'But your thoughts was always too deep for me.'

'The late Mrs Swann never wanted to work,' reflected Swann.

'She was too light and delicate,' said Marsh.

'I would have forbidden it!' said Swann. 'I would never have allowed the disgrace. Men were born to labour, God help them, and women to feel the benefit.'

He looked around and despaired. He was too old to have any hope for himself or the world. The new century, that had seemed, at first, to promise such progress, was lurching like a drunkard down a spiral staircase towards its own destruction.

What will become of a world where the cities roar like factories and the streets are filled with motor cars? The age of machines! No room now for men and horses. Every street a thundering procession of motor buses, motor cycles, motor cars and traction engines. And when all the streets are filled with machines they build new streets and new bridges and more machines to fill them with smoke and noise and danger. And the earth beneath the streets filled with tunnels filled with electric trains. No need to ask a p'liceman! Underground to anywhere. Quickest way. Cheapest fare. And the sky above the streets filled with aeroplanes filled with God-knows-what ready to fall on your head in flames. And no end to the machines or this craving for speed, as if men were doomed to spin in circles, faster and faster, until the planet itself is spun from its orbit. And in the future the world turned into one mighty machine, where men are born into slavery and chained like spokes in the engine wheels. Men made into machines.

Women, too, if they get half a chance.

35

At the beginning of November Violet Askey was walking through Piccadilly towards a meeting of the Working Womens' League. She was forty-five years old. A gaunt, grey-haired woman in a felt hat and a threadbare coat. She carried a carpet bag under her arm and a Votes for Women badge pinned to her coat. The bag contained a brick she had filched from a building site in Soho Square. It was a cold evening, the streets empty, the buildings marooned in a deep, brown, freezing fog. The brick was heavy and Violet was tired.

She was tired because she was growing a cancer. On that dark November evening in 1913 the tumour was the size of a walnut, a small stain at the base of her neck. She would take to her bed in another few weeks and within six months she'd be dead. Had she known of her fate she might not have thrown the brick. She might not have bothered with political meetings, worked for a tyrant like Mrs Nottingham, lived on steamed noodles or died a virgin. But Violet Askey knew nothing. She thought she would live for ever.

She turned a corner and saw the figure of a man on the opposite side of the street. He was a large, bearded man stooping to lock the door of a shop, searching his pockets for keys.

The sight of him made her blood run cold. She stopped walking and stared at this strange yet familiar figure in old-fashioned frock-coat and muffler. And, as she watched, all the frustration of the years, all the regrets and disappointments, overwhelmed her senses and made her go for the brick. She balanced its weight in the palm of her hand, hesitated for a moment or more, and then she threw it at Kingdom Swann's head.

The brick clipped his ear, the window exploded and he fell

to his knees under thousands of flying daggers of glass. When he recovered from the shock and turned to look for his assailant Violet Askey was already gone, running to her death through the gravy-coloured fog.

Cromwell Marsh, who had left the shop only moments before, came running back to the scene of the crime, alarmed by the sound of breaking glass. He found Swann sprawled in the gutter.

'The suffragettes!' gasped Swann. 'The suffragettes are coming!'

'Where?' shouted Marsh.

'There!' shouted Swann, pointing at nothing. His hands and face were covered in blood.

Marsh stared blindly into the fog. 'Did you see them?'

'No,' said Swann. 'They sprang at me from nowhere, screaming and shouting like devils.'

'How many?' said Marsh, afraid that they might return for a second, more violent attack. 'How many of them?'

'Dozens,' groaned Swann. 'There must have been a dozen or more. Great big buggers armed with sticks.'

'You're bleeding,' said Marsh, kneeling down beside him.

'My God!' gasped Swann. 'I've been murdered.'

Marsh pulled out his handkerchief and dabbed at the old man's face. 'How are you feeling?' he asked as he gingerly searched the beard for splinters of window glass.

'I feel very queer,' confessed Swann. His eyebrows had been torn but the heavy muffler had saved him from any serious damage.

'Keep your pecker up,' said Marsh, hauling him out of the gutter and propping him, for safety, against a convenient lamp post. 'We'll soon have you made more comfortable.'

'No hospitals,' wheezed Swann, staring in alarm at his bloody hands. 'I'm too old for hospitals. The doctors will put an end to me...'

'No hospitals,' promised Marsh and, once he'd found a neighbour who would volunteer to guard the shop, he walked Swann home through the fog.

When they reached the house they were greeted by Alice who opened the door and fell back and screamed and started a great commotion. Ethel ran from the parlour, caught sight of her master and had hysterics. Old Mrs Spooner came tottering up from the scullery. The children crawled from the woodwork and stared at the mess on the carpet.

'We was attacked!' announced Marsh breathlessly, setting Swann down at the foot of the stairs. 'Attacked by mad women in the street!' He sent Ethel to run for towels and hot water and asked Alice to help him put Swann to bed.

The old photographer's face was grey, his nose was blue and his eyebrows were black with congealing blood. He looked like a corpse that had been very badly embalmed. He looked very much like Rupert Gladstone's mistress.

'I don't like the colour of him,' said Alice as they laid him out on the counterpane. 'We should call the doctor. He ought to be taken to the hospital.'

'No,' snapped Marsh. 'I promised him. I promised to bring him home. He wanted to die in his own bed. That was his last request.'

'Take off his boots,' said Ethel as she set to work sponging the blood from his hands.

'I think we should keep his feet warm,' argued Alice.

Swann opened his eyes and moaned. 'Faith ...' he whispered, clutching at Ethel's wrist.

'What?' whimpered Ethel. She dropped the sponge and watched in horror as it bounced through the dust beneath the bed.

'I think he wants us to pray,' whispered Alice, dropping to her knees and propping her elbows against the mattress. She screwed up her eyes along with her courage and began to mutter the Lord's Prayer.

'Faith,' said Swann, very weakly. 'Where's Faith? Don't let her see me in this sad state...'

'That's the late Mrs Swann!' exclaimed Marsh, startled at hearing her name again. He took it as a sign that Swann's condition was grave. 'He's confused,' he whispered. 'He's starting to ramble.'

'He's slipping away,' sobbed Ethel, jumping up and kicking the bowl of water.

'Talk to him,' urged Marsh. 'Try to keep him talking.'

'Mr Swann!' shouted Alice. 'This is Alice speaking – you've had a very nasty accident!' She reached out and squeezed his wrist, vainly searching for his pulse with her thumb.

'Do you think he can hear you?' said Ethel, hiding her face in her hands and peeking at Swann through her blood-stained fingers.

'I don't know,' frowned Alice, shaking her head.

'Try again,' insisted Marsh. 'It's not too late. Try and call him back again.'

'Mr Swann!' shouted Alice. 'This is Alice speaking…'

But Swann had fallen asleep.

36

'I could have been killed,' grumbled Swann the next day, as he watched Cromwell Marsh set to work with the broom.

'You've had a very narrow escape,' agreed Marsh, who'd begun to believe the old man must be indestructible.

'It's not safe on the streets!'

'We'll soon get this place working again,' said Marsh, brushing out glass from the floorboards. The door was locked. The shop window had been barricaded against any further attacks.

'No more work,' said Swann, shaking his battered head. 'I want to die in a comfortable bed.' His eyebrows were thick, black, hairy scabs. A thumb and two fingers were bandaged.

'Mustn't be frightened of a few rogue women,' said Marsh.

'It's not the women that frighten me. It's the times,' said Swann. 'I'm an old man. I don't have the energy for all this pandemonium.' He leaned against the counter and turned up his collar to shield his face from the draughts.

Everything changing. The French filling London with foreign postcards. Cheap and nasty titillations. Cardboard keyholes. Petticoat peepshows. Frenchified nudes at sixpence a dozen. They'll soon give them out as cigarette cards. No one cares now for Biblical Beauties. It's all finished. Time to go home and sleep by the fire.

'How long have we been working here?'

'I don't know,' said Marsh.

'I bought this place in 1849,' said Swann gloomily. Two years before the Great Exhibition. I was twenty-four years old and I thought I was a painter. God forgive me, I hoped to be president of the Academy. When I married Mrs Swann, and that was '73, I was already serving behind a camera.

'A long time,' admitted Marsh. 'A lifetime of dedication. Be careful – you're treading on glass.'

'It seems like another world,' sighed Swann. 'It was nothing but wet plates in those days. Your fingers stained black with silver nitrate and your eyes always full of the flash-powder smoke. Now they have celluloid films in rolls and cameras no bigger than notebooks. Everyone owns a camera. You can't walk down the street without meeting someone taking a snap of a horse, a house or a pile of shit. What do they *do* with those pictures?'

'I dare say it's the novelty with some of them tiny cameras,' said Cromwell Marsh.

'Novelty, is it!' barked Swann. 'So that's what became of the world's most influential invention. In Hamburg, thirty years ago, they felt so frightened of the machine they banned photographs of nudes. They banned photographs of *paintings* of nudes! Now any man who owns a Kodak owns twenty-five photographs of his wife undressed down to her short and curlies. Nude knitting. Nude drinking tea. Nude reading *Home Chat* in carpet slippers. What can you make of it?'

'That's socialism,' grinned Marsh. 'The world is changing.'

'I'm tired of the changing. I was happier with the past.'

'You can't walk backward into the future,' said Cromwell Marsh. 'You'll miss the opportunities if you're always looking into the past.' He set down the broom and searched his pockets for cigarettes.

'The past is the future. What happens tomorrow was already decided yesterday. Cause and effect. You don't know where you're going unless you look back over your shoulder.'

Marsh looked disheartened.

'It's different for you,' said Swann gently. He drew up a little bamboo chair that was set aside for customers and squatted down beside the door. 'A young man like you can look to the future with something approaching excitement. Take the studio, with my blessing, and seize your damn opportunities.'

'And where would I find such an artist,' said Marsh, 'as might hope to imitate the lovely visions of your own majestic imagination? There's no artist in London could hope to capture the spirit of your noble nudes! Do you want to break my heart? No, no, it's quite impossible! I'd rather set fire to the whole damn business and toss myself to its flames!' He lit a cigarette and flicked the match to the floor.

'It's no good,' sighed Swann. 'I'm worn out. You must do as you want.' He stood up and ambled through the back of the shop into the silent studio. Marsh followed him, trailing the broom.

'It's nothing without you,' said Marsh, 'and I can't pretend that it's otherwise.' It was cold. Frost against the windows and a stove full of yesterday's ashes.

'And what will you do with yourself when I'm gone?' said Swann. He was grateful, at least, that Marsh had not suggested the introduction of a younger man.

Marsh was silent for a long time. 'I was thinking of nickelodeons,' he said at last. He was fascinated by the moving pictures, knew the names of all the actors and followed the newsreels with interest. Here men were seen to run about the flickering screen, silently shouting, waving their arms, full of self-importance. Ships were launched. Flags were raised. Mobs marched and cavalry charged. So much animation!

'The picturedrome?' said Swann.

'That's it,' said Marsh, walking through the racks of scenery. He paused at a painted window on a peeling canvas wall. 'Everybody wants moving pictures. There's nothing like it. You see the people up there on the screen and they look so real you expect them to talk.' He peered through the window at a Persian garden full of strange and wonderful birds.

'What do *you* know about such things!' scoffed Swann.

'I've made a few enquiries,' said Marsh. 'There's a company in Cricklewood as might welcome a small investment.'

Swann had never see the moving pictures, having heard they injured the eyes. 'You'll be throwing your money away,' he warned.

'Films is the future,' said Marsh, emerging from the Persian garden. 'There's no stopping it.'

'The *Titanic* was the future,' said Swann. 'The future can sink without trace.'

But Cromwell Marsh only smiled and sucked on the stump of his cigarette. He had gone to great pains to secure his own future. He had laid down the plans many months ago when he'd sensed the old man had come to the end of his natural working life. Everything was ready and waiting. There was only one question left to him. 'What will become of the studio?'

'Sell it,' shrugged Swann. He had a notion he might paint again. But this time he'd not suffocate in the dusty air of a studio, mixing his oils with flattery, counting the chins on wealthy matrons. He pictured himself on the beach at Brighton, painting cold, empty stretches of sea.

'And the camera?'

'Sell it!' shouted Swann, turning on his heel and walking away. 'Sell everything. I've finished!'

37

It is with much regret, Marsh informed the subscribers, that the Swann studio, after many years, now feels obliged to close the door on its golden pavilion of pleasure. We thank our faithful friends for their generous support and trust they have always found satisfaction. It was ever our grand ambition to furnish the artist, the connoisseur and the armchair adventurer with views of Womankind that might kindle the heart and excite the sensibilities. And if we succeeded, in any measure, to cast the light of a woman's true beauty into the darkness of the world, we may count ourselves the most fortunate of men and retire from the stage contented.

There were more than a thousand photographs remaining in the stockroom. Cromwell Marsh packed them and sent them direct to Lord Hugo Prattle, in the hope that they might fit his library.

The glass plates, of which there were nearly fifteen thousand, were sold to Godiva Imperial, a successful Haymarket publishing house, who intended to publish the work, at their own discretion, in strictly limited editions. The owner of Godiva was a dubious individual by the name of Clarence Clark. Marsh didn't like the look of him but Clark seemed so anxious to own the plates and offered such vast sums of money, that Cromwell Marsh was persuaded.

Swann was happy and flattered to know that the best of his work would continue to be published. One day, perhaps, when he was long dead and gone, the world might recover its senses and judge his nudes, with an unjaundiced eye, as elemental paintings forged from sunlight and shadow. He had made arrangements, if Marsh should fail to find them a home, to store the plates in his cellar.

The building was put up for sale and all the equipment sent out for auction. The studio, with its wooden stage and fine north window, attracted a number of side-show proprietors in search of London premises. Marsh sold out to a character called Captain Bones who exhibited waxwork cannibals.

38

Swann went home and settled down to a life of leisure. It was 1914. While he sat and toasted his feet by the fire, suffragettes attacked the paintings in the National Gallery and burned down Yarmouth's Britannia Pier. They stoned politicians in the street and jeered at His Majesty the King. A bomb exploded in Westminster Abbey. He followed the rumpus in the evening papers with all the detachment of great old age and fell asleep in his favourite chair. The suffragettes had lost their power to outrage his sensibilities. Nothing surprised him. He was eighty-nine years old. This, alone, astonished him.

It seemed to him that he'd grown so old he should be dead. There were times when he thought he was dead. Without the demands of the studio to occupy his days he began, at once, to feel his years. He was growing deaf. His elbows and knees had rusted away. There were some days when he felt so bad he couldn't find the strength to leave his bed. He drifted now between life and sleep. Ethel cooked him puddings and Alice dosed him with Doctor Mountjoy's Famous Gripe Water which, taken in generous quantities, contained enough milk of opium to soothe the pain in his arms and legs.

Marsh attended the bedside whenever he came to town. He had invested all his money in the British All-Star Vitascope Company, making two-reeler comedies from a converted cattle-shed in Cricklewood. Within a month of his arrival the company had been persuaded to produce the first of its Venus films featuring Pansy Waters, the popular circus star. Pansy, dressed as a scullery-maid, catches her petticoats in the mangle. The mangle explodes. Her frock falls apart. Pansy falls down in confusion. The film had been such a success that Marsh had been given the task of writing and directing a series of fifteen Venus adventures and was always in search of amusing ways for Pansy to be robbed of her clothes.

'They say I'll double my money in less than five years,' he bragged, chewing on a small cigar. He enjoyed his visits. He was nearly sixty years old himself but an afternoon spent with Kingdom Swann made him feel like a boy again. The poor old bugger looked terrible.

'You should have done it years ago,' whispered Swann. 'You shouldn't have listened to an old man.'

'You might be right. You might be wrong,' said Cromwell Marsh. 'But I don't regret a moment. I can thank God I worked with one of the world's great artists. It was my privilege and pleasure to help bare the bums of London's most lovely women. I've seen some sights and no mistake. Every picture was a masterpiece. Every one a coconut. Why, I shouldn't be surprised if they don't decide to build you a museum.'

'A museum?' smiled Swann, trying to imagine the galleries and the colonnades.

'I shouldn't be surprised,' said Marsh. 'A museum of natural beauty. The most lovely women of the century displaying all the good Lord gave 'em in very artistic attitudes.'

'There's been nothing like it in history,' said Swann.

'It would be a scientific phenomenon,' said Marsh. 'A national library of the female nude.'

Swann grunted. 'There'll soon be no women left fit for nudes,' he said sadly. 'Have you seen 'em? Swaggering up and down the streets. Smoking pipes. Dressed like men. Where's the sense to it?'

'They're queer times,' said Marsh.

'What?' shouted Swann.

'Queer times!' roared Marsh.

'Time I was gone,' said Swann, sinking back into the pillows.

'You need some fresh air,' said Marsh, blowing a smoke ring at the ceiling. 'Buy yourself a little motor and get Alice to drive you about the place. It's not healthy to stay in bed. It gives the germs a chance to settle.'

155

'I'm learning to be old,' said Swann. 'I'm a man staring into the twilight.'

'You'll learn nothing in bed,' said Marsh.

But Swann was already falling asleep. His dreams were full of ghostly women. Spirits and sprites, seraphs and sirens. From the far shores of death they gathered to call out and beckon him into the marble halls of his fabulous mausoleum.

As the weeks passed he grew more and more reluctant to be stirred from Doctor Mountjoy's opium dream. He felt comfortable and serene. *The Artist Takes His Leave* of *Creation*. He saw himself sliding gracefully from the withered remains of his body and floating out to heaven.

And then it happened. He was woken one morning by the sound of marching soldiers. Children shouting. Dogs barking. A brass band playing beneath the window. He screwed up his eyes and pulled the bedclothes over his head. But it was no good. The noise continued. Swann was infuriated. He wasn't going to die to the tune of a marching band. He dressed and went down to breakfast.

'What's happening to the world?' he shouted at Ethel as he savaged a plate of scrambled eggs. A child wandered out of the scullery and settled itself at the old man's feet. Swann peered down at the little face. The child grinned back at Swann and chewed the head from a clothes-peg doll.

'It's the Kaiser causing a stink,' Ethel said cheerfully. 'The Germans are in France, the Russians are in Germany and we'll soon be in the thick of it.' She was pleased to see him in such a fine temper. He looked quite restored as he sat in his chair at the kitchen table. His ears blazed and his whiskers bristled.

'Fighting the Frenchie?' he shouted, spitting egg the length of his beard. 'Are we off to fight the French?'

'No,' said Ethel. 'This time we're out to stop the Kaiser.'

'But he's at war with 'em,' he said, sucking at a finger of toast.

'That's it,' said Ethel.

Swann frowned and shook his head. He didn't like the sound of it. 'My father fought the Frenchies. Napoleon damn near blew his head off. We don't owe *them* any favours.'

'I *think* we're helping the French,' said Ethel, growing confused. 'Alice knows more about it. She's been reading the newspaper.'

'We can't be helping the Russians!' said Swann.

Alice came into the kitchen nursing a pail of milk. 'What are you doing out of bed?' she scolded when she saw her master at the table.

'I can't rest for the noise in the street,' grumbled Swann. 'Ethel says we're at war with the Kaiser.'

'That's nothing to worry your head about,' said Alice. 'It will all be finished before it gets started.'

'How's that?' said Ethel.

'They say we're going to war at sea,' announced Alice. 'There's to be a battle as big as Trafalgar.'

'Nonsense!' said Swann.

'You wait,' said Alice. 'We're out to sink the German fleet!'

'How do you know?' said Ethel.

'It's general knowledge,' said Alice. 'We've built the biggest dreadnoughts in the history of the world. Armour-plated battleships so fast that they can't be hit and so strong that they can't be sunk. I was reading about them yesterday.'

'All the more reason for the Kaiser to keep his fleet at home,' said Swann, wiping the egg from his beard.

'I don't understand you,' said Alice. 'Why build battleships if you can't use 'em? It's a waste of money. It doesn't make sense.' She set the pail upon the table and wiped the hair from her eyes. She looked big and strong and confident. She had a little paper Union Jack pinned to her apron pocket.

The next day, to no one's surprise, Great Britain declared war on Germany. London and Berlin erupted with scenes of jubilation. Ten thousand gathered before Buckingham Palace to throw their hats in the air for the King. The streets echoed to the pipes and drums. Volunteers stormed recruiting offices. The troop trains stood waiting at Waterloo Station.

'Isn't it fun!' laughed Ethel. 'It's just like the Coronation.'

'And don't they look lovely in uniform,' sighed Alice, brushing a tear from her eye.

Swann could find no peace in the house. In the warmth of an August afternoon he went strolling as far as Westminster. The cavalry were camped in St James's Park. There were soldiers marching on the lawns and horses grazing the flower beds. It looked so much like a Mountjoy dream that the old man stopped, for a minute, to stare. And there, in the shade of a tree, he saw a group of Piccadilly suffragettes. They wore bonnets sewn with paper flowers and cheerful summer frocks. They were laughing and calling to the crowd. Whenever a young man came within range they ran forward and thrust a pamphlet into his hand. This pamphlet, boldly printed in red and blue, illustrated with a demon Kaiser and still smelling sweetly of the printer's ink, pleaded with men to 'Leave Home & Fight!'

39

'Suffragettes? Good luck to them, sir,' said Mrs Beeton over afternoon tea. 'It's more work for the pleasure houses. If there were no suffragettes in the world God would have to invent 'em. The more women out there throwing bombs and talking politics the better for business.' She smiled and brushed biscuit crumbs from her skirt.

'And why do they seem so anxious for war?' demanded Swann. 'They're marching through town like recruiting sergeants.'

'I'm surprised you ask such a question! A war suits their purposes to perfection. There's nothing like it for making money or fanning the flames of revolution.'

'Revolution, is it?' said Swann.

Mrs Beeton poured him more tea from a large, ornate, silver pot. It was clear that she thought of herself as a fully emancipated woman. She was wealthy, independent and industrious. She was also very proud of her girls and looked after them, encouraging them to save their money to provide for the comforts required in old age. They could read and write and conduct a spirited conversation with anyone from a king to a coster. They studied the bible and some of them sang in the church on Sundays. They were kept in the very pink of health and constantly examined, for pleasure, by the best of the London surgeons. They wanted for nothing and their only fear was of persecution by the militant suffragettes. Mrs Beeton had a poor opinion of the suffragettes.

'I hear them banging the drum for social justice,' she said. 'It's not justice they want, Mr Swann. They want power. And because it's the men that hold the power they call those men wicked and corrupt. But it's the power that corrupts and makes 'em so wicked. And when women finally grasp the power there will be not a ha'pence of difference.'

'I don't like it,' said Swann. 'Women dressed as men.'

'Pay 'em no heed,' said Mrs Beeton, hoping to soothe him. 'I've known men who like to dress as women.'

'What?' roared Swann.

'It's true, sir! Full-grown men in silk stockings and little chemises, prancing around with their pokers out.'

'Sodomites!' gasped Swann.

'Dear me, I don't believe they betrayed such inclinations in *this* house, Mr Swann, or I'm sure I would have noticed it,' she said, prodding her hair. 'In matters of hygiene I'm most particular.'

'What other sort of man would take to wearing petticoats?' demanded Swann.

'Important men. Influential men. All of them born to the ruling classes. If they weren't in such positions of power they'd be scrubbing floors in the madhouse,' she declared and paused to nibble a sugared biscuit. 'Women in trousers. Men in skirts. There's nothing to choose between them.'

The world is changing too fast, thought Swann. There's nothing can be trusted. He had celebrated the women of a golden age, undraped and untroubled, *in puris naturalibus*. And many of these fleeting nudes with their high breasts and fatted calves were already gone from the world, withered like summer roses, transmigrated into grey-skinned matrons, whiskers sprouting from their chins and the light gone from their eyes.

He had cheated death a thousand times, stolen women's reflections in a miracle of mirrors and fixed them for all eternity, in praise of beauty, for the pleasure of man and the greater glory of God. The enduring songs of love! *O, pubis magnificat!* He had made these women immortal. Each brief blush of beauty had made its small, indelible impression. A simple testament of joy to set against the terrors of life.

He should never have sold the collection. Fashions change. Nothing was constant. Photographs spoil. Glass plates were broken. How long would it take before most of his work could be counted as lost or destroyed? He must have been mad! Why had Marsh persuaded him? Who were those wretched Haymarket men? He resolved to visit their warehouse to satisfy himself that his work was properly stored and secured.

'Retrieve your pictures at any cost!' said the admirable Mrs Beeton. 'How could you bear to part with them? You've a duty to leave them for the nation.'

'The nation doesn't want them,' grieved Swann.

'It makes no difference. The nation don't know what it wants. I've half a mind to purchase the plates myself.'

'You flatter me, ma'am, and I thank you for it,' said Swann

'Flatter you?' said Mrs Beeton, snapping her biscuit. 'Flatter you, my arse! I've an eye for a work of art, Mr Swann. You can't sell *me* a wooden nutmeg. One day your pictures will be historical. They're important. They're unique. I guarantee, we'll not see the likes of them again. I should have been proud to have taken charge of them. It wounds me to think that you never allowed me such an opportunity.'

'By God, you shall have them!' he cried, stamping his foot and making the tea cup jump from its saucer. 'They couldn't find a better home. I'll go there and fetch 'em myself.'

But he was too late.

40

Late on a Friday afternoon the police raided the Haymarket office of Godiva Imperial and arrested Clarence Clark. He had been accused of keeping children for the purpose of prostitution. Although he was innocent of the charge, he broke beneath their interrogation and confessed to a dozen other crimes. *One:* he was guilty of offering for sale a range of indecent clockwork novelties designed to corrupt public morals. *Two:* he was responsible for the manufacture of a notorious aphrodisiac called Casanova drops which, when introduced to a victim's food, poisoned the stomach and irritated the bowels. *Three:* he also pleaded guilty to selling a dangerous preparation made from a mixture of camphor and mustard and known as Old Stallion embrocation. *Four:* he had ordered, from somewhere in Germany, a range of giant dildoes and leather bondage equipment. *Five:* he had sold rubber masks and stockings and items of waterproof underwear. *Six:* he had offered a quantity of X-ray spectacles that he claimed could render women naked through the thickest protective garments. *Seven:* he had lied about these spectacles. *Eight:* he had offered bad translations of forbidden continental novels. *Nine:* he had written most of these novels himself under several different names. *Ten:* he had published the ancient Egyptian method of hypnotising reluctant women, satisfaction guaranteed. *Eleven:* he had printed a monthly directory of London's most comfortable brothels. *Twelve:* he had organised the sale of an unknown number of pornographic photographs and drawings.

In a back room at Vine Street police station Clarence Clark wept and begged for mercy. He pleaded insanity. He asked them to think of his crippled mother. He offered them a substantial reward to forget their investigations.

The police were not impressed.

Once they knew the nature of the publishing business they wasted no time in breaking into the warehouse. The building was stuffed, from floor to ceiling, with bundles of photographs, prints and novels. They had never seen such a wicked hoard of human degradation. The bonfires burned for a week. Swann's master collection was destroyed, along with a shipment of loathsome French postcards, several thousand lewd woodblock prints recently shipped from Japan and a set of pornographic etchings by Pablo Picasso of Paris.

41

'You can take some more snaps, Mr Swann,' said Ethel.
'I'll show you my bum,' said Alice.

Kingdom Swann lay in bed with his beard combed over his nightgown. He didn't move nor make a sound. His face was a mask of despair. He refused all food and drank only from Mountjoy's poisoned bottle. After three or four days with no improvement Cromwell Marsh was summoned from his offices at Cricklewood.

'I don't like the look of him, sir,' said Alice, as she hurried him up the stairs.

'Have you called the doctor?'

'He won't let no doctor tamper with him,' puffed Alice. 'He won't even let Ethel change the sheets on his bed. We tried to bath him on Sunday night but he kicked and struggled and put up such a terrible fight we couldn't hold him and let him go back to bed half-washed and used the hot water ourselves since we didn't want it wasted.'

'Are you feeding him?' said Marsh, who had brought along a bowl of calf's foot jelly, wrapped in a muslin cloth.

'We can't make him eat a morsel,' said Alice. 'He's taken out his teeth.'

When they entered the room they found Swann in his dressing gown, standing, staring, through an open window.

Marsh glanced at him apprehensively, sat down in a chair, placed the bowl of jelly at his feet and perched his hat on his knees. For some time the two men shared the room in silence. A draught from the window shook the lace curtains. Beside the bed a little clock began to chime.

'There are women out there running riot,' murmured Kingdom Swann, 'slashing pictures of famous men.' He turned from the window and glowered at Marsh. 'And now there are men breaking doors down with hammers and making bonfires of women. And all around them the world at war, the whole damn world going up in flames!' He was shrieking, his face full of thunder and his red eyes rolling. 'I should never have lived so long! Never! Never! God should have spared me from this!' He hobbled up and down the room, wringing his hands and blowing savagely through his whiskers.

'There's nothing to be done,' said Marsh miserably, torturing his hat. 'It's a terrible misfortune but there's nothing to be done…' He knew the whole, sad story but had hoped that the news might be kept from Swann. It was enough to break the old man's heart.

'They threw my life on the fire!' roared Swann. 'And you tell me there's nothing to be done!'

'What have you lost?' argued Cromwell Marsh. 'Plates we've printed a thousand times. It makes no difference to your reputation. Your work is everywhere. Why, there's most likely a Kingdom Swann nude in every artistic household in England. I shouldn't be surprised if your photographs was admired in the distant outposts of Empire!'

'Scattered and gone,' moaned Swann. 'Blown to the wind. That's the truth of it.'

'But you must have your own collection,' said Marsh. 'A few of your personal favourites…'

'I don't have a collection,' wept Swann.

'You kept nothing?' said Marsh, surprised. He had hoarded every picture of Alice the studio had published and even secretly printed from plates that Swann had ordered to be destroyed because of some fault in the composition. He owned more views of Alice Hancock than any man alive and never grew tired of studying them. He especially prized the snaps of Alice caught unprepared, bending with her eyes half-closed and her drawers pulled open between her knees. The chance exposure, the stolen glance, had always excited him more than any formal arrangement. He kept his pictures of Alice in a box at the back of the wardrobe. He called it his private collection.

'Why should I collect my own work?' said Swann bitterly. 'God forbid, but I trusted you to take care of all that!'

'I didn't know…' said Marsh. 'I thought I'd done you proud. The man had an excellent reputation.'

'You ruined me!' barked Swann.

Marsh punched his hat and looked forlorn. He'd been wrong about Clarence Clark. The man was a fraud and a scoundrel. They were lucky to have escaped his fate: in a bid to save his own skin he might well have had them all arrested. Marsh shuddered. 'We could write to all the old customers and explain your unhappy circumstance,' he suggested. 'Some of them early pictures is worth a pretty penny. We'll buy 'em back.'

'What?'

'We'll buy 'em back!' shouted Marsh. 'Certainly. Give it twelve months and you'll find we've recovered the whole collection.'

'I'm a hundred years old!' raved Swann. 'Why can't I make you understand? I can't wait twelve months. I can't wait twelve *weeks*. I might drop dead this afternoon!'

Marsh couldn't argue with him. The old man looked ready to burst his nose. He stared miserably around the room. The silence settled. He couldn't find any more words of comfort. He wondered if he should mention the bowl of calf's foot jelly. He decided against it and pushed it deeper under the chair with a gentle sweep of his foot.

And then, in a moment of desperation, he remembered Lord Hugo Prattle. The private museum at Prattle House contained the largest surviving hoard of Kingdom Swann's work in the country. The collection had lately been neglected since, unknown to the great photographer, Marsh had introduced his lordship to the pleasures of moving picture shows. Prattle had spared no expense to fit out his bedroom with all the necessary equipment and now spent his days in bed, watching naked chorus girls flitter like ghosts on the walls. This new novelty consumed all his time and energy and the library gathered dust. He would telephone his lordship and ask him to open the library for Swann.

42

When Prattle heard the story he wrote, at once, to Kingdom Swann and begged him to make haste for Dorset. The photographer would be his permanent guest, a suite of rooms would be made available and the entire collection of books, prints, paintings and photographs put at his disposal. It would be Lord Hugo Prattle's privilege to have the great artist as guardian of the library.

'Imagine it!' said Cromwell Marsh, when he read the letter aloud to his master. 'You've been given the keys to the Prattle library. He wants to put you in charge of the greatest collection of nudes in Europe. What do you think of that!' He lit a small cigar and beamed down at the ancient photographer, who was laid out in bed with his head propped up by a pillow. He was feeling very pleased with himself. He was waiting for Swann's congratulations.

'I think it's a scandal,' grumbled Swann. 'Making me go out and beg for the pleasure of viewing my work. At my age the artist should be at home, sitting beside a blazing fire, surrounded by the loving attention of women and children and big-bellied dogs. He shouldn't be sent out into the cold and driven hundreds of miles from his hearth whenever he wants to look at his pictures.' He closed his eyes and pretended to fall asleep.

'It's no distance,' protested Marsh. 'And I never before heard you mention dogs.'

'It's a long expedition to undertake at my time of life,' murmured Swann. 'Travel shakes up the bones and puts a fearful strain on the stomach. Anything could happen. My heart gives out or my bladder bursts and they'd find me dead on arrival…' He raised his hand, very weakly, and wagged it at

Marsh as if he were waving goodbye to the world.

'Nonsense,' said Marsh. 'You'll enjoy it. An excursion will do you a power of good and these days the railways are excellent.'

'I never much cared for Dorset,' sighed Swann. 'It's nothing but beasts and wilderness and all the roads are made of mud.'

'You'll be living in a palace,' said Marsh, snapping his fingers against the letter. 'Prattle was never a man to deprive himself of the comforts. Properly appointed rooms. Big, healthy country girls acting as maids. Six meals a day and nothing to do with your time but sleep in the sun and grow fat.'

'Rich food,' yawned Swann. 'Rich food never agreed with me.' He closed his eyes again and settled his head in the pillow.

Cromwell Marsh lost his patience. He jumped up and walked to the window, snorting ribbons of smoke through his nose. What was wrong with the silly old bugger? Why was he proving so difficult? 'You can't decline such an honour!' he said, chewing impatiently on his cigar. 'It's quite unthinkable. Why, it would be like refusing a knighthood!'

Swann was quickly persuaded, although he wouldn't admit it to Marsh. If he wanted to see his work again he would have to accept Prattle's invitation. The thought of the library excited him and restored him to the land of the living. He came off Mountjoy's bottle and let Alice give him a bath. He found his teeth and sank them into a hot beef pudding.

When the time came he left the house near Golden Square in the care of Ethel and Alice. He had given them the property, although they didn't know it yet, and made them secure with generous pensions. He settled the greater part of his fortune on the five Spooner children to provide them with proper educations, gave old Mrs Spooner a beer allowance and deposited a small sum for the upkeep of his wife's grave at Highgate cemetery. He was furtive about these arrangements and discussed them with no one beyond the solicitor's office. He hoped to return to London at some time in the future but at his age, and in his poor health, he would not undertake the journey without his affairs in good order.

Ethel and Alice were very upset at the news of their master's departure. They knew they would never see him again. On the morning of his departure they were up before dawn, warming his vest, shining his boots and snorting into their handkerchiefs.

'You'll write a postcard when you arrive,' said Alice, looking very flushed as she carried his suitcases down the stairs. She leaned towards him to plant a kiss but only managed to bend his nose.

Swann said that he would write postcards to all of them and Dorset wasn't very far away and these days the railways were excellent and he'd probably want to come home in a week.

'I made a meat and pickle pie for the journey,' said Ethel, running breathlessly from the kitchen. 'But the crust caught and I threw it away.' She looked at Swann, then burst into tears and pulled her apron over her head.

Swann tried to comfort her but only succeeded in making her worse and after she'd daubed his face with kisses she fled to hide in the larder.

'Look after Ethel for me,' he whispered, turning to Alice and then, to his great embarrassment, Alice burst into tears and crushed him roughly into her arms, making him wheeze and fight for breath.

When he reached the front door old Mrs Spooner lined up the children to shake him by the hand. He gave them each an aniseed ball. Mrs Spooner smacked her gums and brushed away a tear.

'You're a lovely, lovely gent, Mr Swann.'

43

When Kingdom Swann climbed down from the train at Upshott Magna he found Lord Hugo Prattle waiting for him with the station master and a brace of porters. His lordship, face hidden by a pair of goggles, flapped forward in a long canvas coat and embraced Swann so enthusiastically that the old man fell back and tumbled over his luggage. The porters picked him up, the station master brushed him down and, when he was quite recovered, his lordship led him to a motor car that was parked in the station yard.

'Came to collect you myself,' he said proudly, banging the bonnet with his fist. 'Trained a groom to drive this brute. Lost him last month. All the young men go to war. House full of women.'

He hauled Swann into the passenger seat and wrapped his legs in a blanket. It was a foreign racing-machine. A green metal fish on wheels. Prattle climbed behind the controls, wiped his goggles with a silk scarf and frowned doubtfully at the steering wheel.

'Is it safe?' asked Swann timidly.

'Safe?' said Prattle, looking puzzled.

'I've never ridden a racer,' said Swann, who had never ridden in a motor car of any description and had hoped to be spared it.

'There's nothing to it,' beamed Prattle. 'It's like sitting in a railway carriage with all the windows open. You'll love it.'

'You hear of such fearful accidents,' said Swann.

'I've never had a collision yet,' laughed Prattle, pulling at the lever he thought might be the brake.

'How long have you been driving?'

'Since eight o'clock this morning.'

Swann was trying to open the door and throw himself overboard when the engine spluttered into life. 'Hold tight!' shouted Prattle and then they were shooting down a gravel road into the winter twilight.

'Too fast!' cried Swann. But his words were swept away in a deafening tunnel of wind. The world was spinning, lurching, melting into fantastic shapes. He closed his eyes. The wind stung his face and drilled his ears. His nose turned a dangerous shade of blue. 'Too fast!' he moaned, shrinking into his seat and pulling the blanket over his head.

Prattle clung to the controls, grinding his teeth in concentration. Birds burst from hedges and fled, shrieking, into the sky. Cattle trumpeted in pens. At a bend in the road a dog, emerging from a ditch, was caught in the wheels and thrown twenty yards through a fence.

'Crazy dog!' screamed his lordship. 'Did you see that? We could have been killed!'

Swann said nothing. It was growing dark. Lamps were burning at cottage windows. The rushing fields were lakes of mud. Despite his love of speed, it took an hour for Prattle to find his way home. He lost his way in the narrow lanes and stopped several times to ask for directions.

'I ought to recognise the land,' he kept shouting. 'It's been in the family for three hundred years!'

At last they found the iron gates that marked the boundary of the estate and splashed through an avenue of skeleton elms towards the lights of the great house.

The entire household had gathered on the steps of the house. Prattle jumped from the car, tore the goggles from his face and waved at the frozen bundle still huddled in the passenger seat.

'This is Mr Kingdom Swann,' he announced. 'The very famous photographer. He is to be our guest. You are here to look after him. The man is a great artist. A genius. We shall never see such a man again. A privilege and a pleasure to have the honour to attend to him.'

The housekeeper stepped forward to drop a curtsey, followed by the cooks, the housemaids, laundry-maids, kitchen-maids, scullery-maids and maids-of-all-work. The maids, who were very young, wore high bustles to their skirts so that, when they moved, they seemed to pitch forward, strutting like fat-breasted turkeys. Mrs Petersen, the housekeeper, was dressed in a gown more suited for the opera than the duties of a country house and cut so low she'd been forced to cover herself with a shawl against the damp night air. Even the cooks, who were nearly as plain as their food, had been turned out in freshly starched aprons and caps. The only men to be seen were four decrepit gardeners who tipped their hats and shuffled their heavy, iron-shod boots as they laboured to unload the luggage.

'Welcome, Mr Swann, to my humble family home,' said Prattle, wrenching open the car door to help Kingdom Swann back to earth. 'We hope to make you most comfortable.' But Swann did not move. He was frozen to the seat. The blanket that covered him sparkled with frost. When Prattle gave the bundle a poke, it toppled reluctantly into his arms.

The cooks, housemaids, laundry-maids, kitchen-maids, scullery-maids and maids-of-all-work shrank away from the scene with a gasp. The gardeners dropped the luggage and gawped. It was left to Mrs Petersen to run down the steps and help carry Swann to the safety of the house. Prattle took his arms, the housekeeper took his legs, and together they hauled him upstairs and laid him out on the bed.

'Is he dead?' whispered Prattle, once they'd unwrapped him and peered at the silent face through the tangled growth of beard.

'No,' said Mrs Petersen. 'His heart is beating. It's very faint but I think I can feel it beating.' She had broken open the old man's waistcoat and was feeling anxiously under his shirt.

'What are we going to do?' moaned Prattle. He paced up and down the room, his canvas coat slapping the furniture. 'Fetch a doctor!' he shouted at no one. 'Bring me a dozen hot water bottles! Give his chest a whisky rub!'

'You must leave him alone with me, sir,' said Mrs Petersen softly. 'I have ways to help revive him.' She had pulled off his boots and was briskly slapping the soles of his feet.

'What?' barked Prattle suspiciously. 'What are you planning to do with him? I don't want any of your damn gymnastics, madam! He's an old man. He's very fragile. He wasn't born in one of your fjords!'

Mrs Petersen rose and stared down at Lord Hugo Prattle with eyes that were full of thunder. She jerked the shawl from her shoulders and flung it to the floor. 'If we do not act quickly, sir, I believe we shall be too late to save him. His blood is freezing under his skin. If we cannot revive him very soon an icicle may puncture his heart.'

This diagnosis was so bizarre and yet uttered with such authority that Prattle was lost for words. He bristled and growled and puffed himself up but he couldn't match his housekeeper's height nor her look of determination. 'Ring the bell if you need assistance!' he snapped, retreating towards the door.

When his lordship finally withdrew Mrs Petersen turned the key in the lock and threw more coals on the fire. She kicked off her shoes and unlaced the front of her gown. She wrenched the gown to her waist and struggled next to unwork her corset, tugging savagely at the cords until she had broken free from the shell.

Swann lay sprawled in the eiderdown with his mouth open and his eyes closed. His breath was reduced to a rattle. She pulled him roughly from his clothes and managed to roll him into bed. His skin was very cold and all the colour had leaked from his face. She paused to listen, again, for his heart. And then she lay down upon him, pressed his face between her breasts and touched him with her living heat.

The frost pierced her body and made her moan with pain. She shivered and clasped the old man tighter, afraid that she might have embraced a ghost. For a long time she shielded him, smothered him, until her own warmth had dwindled away and she felt so chilled she supposed all hope had been lost. But gradually he began to thaw. His ears burned and his big beard steamed. The blood returned to his feet. He grunted and mumbled in his sleep, turning his face to the pillow.

Mrs Petersen slipped from the bed, threw on her gown and quickly searched for her shawl and shoes. When Swann woke up she was gone. He never knew what had happened to him. There was a flask of hot tea beside the bed and a bowl of spiced milk pudding.

Abishag the Shunamite Excites the Old Man's Dreams.

44

The next morning Swann was up early and walking with Prattle beside the lake. He had taken precautions against the cold by wearing two coats and a bear-skin hat but he felt none the worse for the night's ordeal.

'You gave us a nasty fright,' said Prattle, swinging an ebony walking cane. 'We were quite convinced you were dead.'

'The cold,' puffed Swann. 'The cold knocked me out.'

'I don't suppose you remember what happened?' said Prattle hopefully.

'We were sitting in the racer,' said Swann, 'and the next thing I knew…' He paused and scratched his beard. 'I woke up in bed, stark naked and covered in sweat.'

'And you don't remember, ah, Mrs Petersen helping to revive you in any fashion?'

'I don't recall such a thing,' said Swann.

Prattle sighed and looked disappointed.

'Why do you ask?'

'Oh, no reason in particular. Nasty business. Best forgotten. But you'll need to rest, sir, and build up your strength. We can't have you going down queer again.'

'I'm much obliged to you, sir,' said Swann. 'If it wasn't for your kindness I'm sure I don't know how I should have endured so many disappointments.'

'Nonsense!' said Prattle. 'Why, not only do I have the honour of entertaining the most distinguished artist of the age, I find I now possess the largest collection of his work in Christendom.' He laughed and coughed and took Swann's arm.

He led the old man through a bank of rhododendrons and there, half-hidden in the long grass by the shore of the ornamental lake, rose a white marble casket, set on a polished granite block, surrounded by seven, naked, mourning maids.

'Now ain't that a sight for sore eyes, Mr Swann? Don't the look of it warm the blood? I sent to Italy for the sculptor. All the best. No expense spared. He followed your photographs to the smallest detail.' He smiled and gazed up in admiration. 'A woman is a miracle of beauty,' he reflected. 'They do nothing to earn it. Some of 'em frankly despises it. Yet God, in his wisdom, makes 'em lovely and man a slave to the sight of 'em.' He clambered onto the grave and sat astride a prostrate mourner, rubbing the frost from her flanks with his gloves. 'I come down here on summer evenings, rest my head among the bums and lean back to look at the stars,' he said softly, casting a critical glance at the sky.

'You always had a love for women,' said Swann.

'And you the art of praising 'em,' beamed his lordship.

'I should have been a painter,' said Swann sadly, pulling at the collars of his coats.

'How's that?' said Prattle.

'They don't take such a serious view of paint,' said Swann. 'It's the photographs that frightens them.'

'A painting emulates but a photograph stimulates,' said Prattle, clapping his hands. 'That's the difference. It's magic. It's witchcraft. It's stealing from life.'

'I stole nothing!' barked Swann. 'I celebrated women's beauty. Big, fat, honest women, common women, simple women, women made to stir the heart and invigorate the senses. I nearly flooded the world with their beauty. I nearly drowned the world with pleasure. It was a revolution. And now they want to destroy me.'

'Who?' said Prattle, climbing down from the grave. 'Who are they? A few philistines, old maids and tosspots with a morbid dread of their sexual parts.'

'Policemen,' said Swann. 'Damn great policemen armed with hammers.'

'They won't try anything like that here,' snorted Prattle. 'Private property. Everything under lock and key.'

'Did Marsh send you a parcel of pictures?'

'A thousand of 'em!' laughed Prattle. 'All wrapped up to look like Fortnum & Mason hampers. The station master met them and brought them up here in his wagon.'

'I'd like to see them again,' said Swann.

'The library is at your disposal, sir,' said Prattle. He put an arm around the old man and guided him slowly back to the house.

'By thunder, but it's cold!' he exclaimed as he unlocked the heavy, oak doors. The hall was dark and smelt of damp. 'I'll fetch a maid to light the fire and bring you a flask of something hot.'

But Kingdom Swann didn't hear him. He was already wading into the gloom, searching the cobwebs and shadows.

45

He sat beneath the Hindu bronze of the woman and monkey locked in love and surveyed the albums and boxes that stretched the length of the library floor. Here was everything he feared had been lost, from the early sepia portraits of ghostly nudes in silver fog to the recent coloured photographs of red-haired, blue-eyed women with crimson-tipped breasts and blushes on their bountiful buttocks. The complete works of Kingdom Swann. The women he had known and loved and the women he had loved and forgotten. In the pages of a leather album he was reunited with Astor Pilbury, the notorious London beauty, who had broken hearts in Europe, Transvaal and Rajputana; who owned a castle in Spain and a mountain in Scotland; who had paid a fortune to have herself photographed, half-woman, half-fish, a mermaid drowned in a fisherman's net. And here a woman with a name long-forgotten, immortal now as a queen of Persia, naked on a panther skin, head thrown back in pain or pleasure, one breast clasped in a serpent's tail while the monster, with its jaws sprung open, curled out its tongue to nuzzle her notch. Among the rich and famous he found shop-girls and factory-slaves, who had come and gone in drudgery, leaving no mark upon the world, but for these few photographs where their simple beauty shone clear to heaven. And, for Swann, these were not pasteboard fantasies but laborious transformations, suggesting alternative realities, secret identities, a method of scratching at the hard and dirty crust of the world to reveal the beauty beneath its surface. He had taken commonplace women and fashioned them into exquisite objects of desire, erotic seraphim to stir the senses and dazzle the eye. The women were gone, grown old and faded, but their magic influence remained. This was the proof of his alchemy.

46

During the months that followed Swann's arrival at Prattle House a small but distinguished stream of visitors made a pilgrimage to the library. George Augustus Fry was the first to pay his respects. Fry had once owned the London Exhibition Rooms and been considered the foremost rival of Murray Marks, the famous Oxford Street art dealer. During the 1890s he had commissioned Swann to photograph a string of beautiful mistresses. The women had long since been lost, along with their portraits, and he seized this last opportunity to reflect on the triumphs of happier times.

He was followed by Sir Frederick Watson, Alfred Lord Spencer and other patrons of the arts. Prattle spared no expense on the comfort of his guests and the big house became a favourite haunt of the aged dilettante.

At Christmas Cromwell Marsh arrived on the train from London. He appeared at the door, dressed in a wolf-skin coat, with twelve pieces of leather luggage. He had left his wife to enjoy the season's jollifications in the care of their eldest daughter and, at Prattle's request, come down to talk of the old days with Swann. He greeted the photographer with a great deal of affection and brought him news from Golden Square.

'Ethel prospers but Alice is down with a touch of distemper on account of a change in the weather; the children are bigger, the old one is smaller and Gloria has come to stay having quit her room in Old Compton Street being tired, as she says, of a life spent praying with her knees in the air.'

'Do they have enough of everything?' asked Swann, happy to remember them. 'How do they manage in the house?'

'They want for nothing, thanks to your generosity. Ethel has engaged a cook and has every hope of finding a maid. She sends her love, together with Alice and Gloria, and the children send you a box of peg-dolls which I've packed away in my luggage.'

'And Mrs Marsh?'

'Mrs Marsh, may God preserve her pipes and tubes, enjoys a spell of very poor health. You've never seen so many doctors! It's costing me a fortune. They're forever rubbing her chest or sticking their fingers up her bum. She has ointments for every part of the body and pills for every day of the week. She's never enjoyed herself more.'

'And yourself?'

'The Vitascope business never stops growing,' grinned Marsh, 'despite the shortages caused by the war.'

The next day Valentine Crane, the distinguished painter of nudes, who had collected much of Swann's early work and copied the photographs into his paintings, travelled from Cromer to visit the library. He was a heavy, bearded man with hands that had cruelly withered to claws. He showed no remorse for his lifetime of shameless plagiarism and it amused Kingdom Swann to think that his photographs, many of which had been copies of popular paintings, should be forged again as canvases.

Crane's great passion, since he'd grown too old and arthritic to paint, was the modern cinema. At dinner he engaged Cromwell Marsh in long discussions on the merits of motion pictures. He loved Keystone comedies, adventure serials and anything featuring Bronco Billy. He had only recently seen a startling Pathe production in colour.

'A costume drama set in ancient Greece. The flesh tints so natural you'd swear they were living actors performing their parts behind a glass screen,' he told Marsh, who was looking most impressed.

'It's damn clever, eh, Mr Swann?' said Prattle, draining a glass of claret.

Swann was asleep but another of the dinner guests, a famous old sculptor called Spinks, was quite overwhelmed by the news. 'The spectacle!' he cried in excitement. 'Living beauties, lovely in every particular, larking about as bold as brass and into all manner of mischief!' He was a ghost of a man in a baggy suit and a pair of gleaming spectacles. He jumped up, sat down and stuffed his mouth with cheese.

'Little rascals, some of 'em,' grinned Cromwell Marsh.

'Mabel Normand the Diving Venus,' sighed Crane.

'Florence Lawrence the Biograph Girl,' chuckled Marsh.

'The ladies was always a weakness of mine,' said Prattle, wiping his hands on his knees. The table was heaped with holly, apples, nuts and cheeses; bottles of wine, crusts of pies and skeletons of turkeys. He poured himself a glass of claret and belched peacefully.

'It's a miracle of electric light,' declared Cromwell Marsh, turning to smile at Kingdom Swann. 'The wonder of the age.'

'What does he think of Mabel Normand the Keystone Water Nymph?' enquired Crane.

'I don't believe he's had the pleasure,' said Marsh. 'He doesn't hold with the cinema.'

'Wake him up and ask him,' insisted Spinks.

'We was wondering what you thought of the modern bioscope beauty, Mr Swann!' shouted Marsh, shaking the old man awake.

'What?' shouted Swann. 'What?'

'The modern bioscope, Mr Swann,' said Crane. 'We was asking for your opinion.'

Swann, half-buried in a tangle of holly, growled and stuck out his beard. 'It's a cheap trick!' he roared, banging the table with his fist. 'A cheap trick designed to bamboozle half-wits!'

The company fell silent. Prattle set down his glass. Spinks stopped molesting the Stilton.

'I'm surprised to hear you speak so strong, Mr Swann,' ventured Crane, alarmed by the mutiny.

'I've no time for it,' said Swann, wagging his head.

'Did you never see little Mary Pickford?' said Spinks.

'A prodigious beauty,' Prattle confessed. 'She'd melt the marrow in your bones.'

'It strains the eyes,' muttered Swann. 'The eye can't hold the speed of the pictures. Mark my words, it will drive men mad and blind a generation of children.'

'Now that's very queer,' said Crane, pondering a polony. 'Very queer. I should have thought that a man like yourself would have wasted no time in setting his mind to such an invention.'

'How's that?' growled Swann.

'Well, a photograph is a splendid deceit…' said Crane.

'Especially when its subject is a ripe young woman exposing her nether regions,' said Prattle.

'But when that photograph gets up and walks around and stretches and smiles and beckons you forward…' continued Crane.

'That's art!' shouted Spinks.

'It's something to contemplate,' agreed Cromwell Marsh.

'A rare sight,' said Prattle, smacking his lips. He looked very flushed and his eyes were shining.

'The film is dreams brought to life,' said Crane, leaning back in his chair. 'What do *you* say Mr Spinks.'

'I must confess that I've never actually seen one,' said the sculptor, feeling very foolish. 'But I've heard enough to form that opinion.'

'What?' gasped Crane in astonishment.

'I can hardly believe my ears!' said Marsh.

'A man of your experience,' said Crane.

'It can't be helped,' said the sculptor, looking aggrieved. 'I never had the opportunities.'

'I'll soon put a stop to that, sir!' exclaimed Prattle, grinding his teeth with excitement. 'It's an education. No time to waste.' Marsh had brought him the latest All-Star Vitascope production and now he saw his chance to introduce the novelty as part of the evening's entertainments.

'A film show?' said Crane. 'A film show here in the house?'

'Yes, sir! Marsh brings 'em down from London.'

'I has the honour to provide his lordship with certain choice requisites,' toadied Marsh.

'Do you have, by chance, the latest adventures of Bronco Billy?' said Valentine Crane.

'Bugger Bronco Billy!' cried Spinks. 'Bring on the dancing girls!'

47

THE GERMAN SURRENDER!

Lady Wagtail waits for his Lordship

A woman stands at her bedroom window and stares across fields to a view of the sea. The woman is young and beautiful and her gown is so grand, and her arms so plump, that she must be the mistress of the house. She presses a letter to her heart and rolls her lovely eyes to heaven.

Down in the Kitchen

The maids are small and pretty. They are working at a scrubbed table. The first maid washes a rolling pin in a basin of soapy water. Bracelets of bubbles hang from her wrists. The second maid sets out to polish a set of silver candlesticks. She is laughing and showing her teeth. The third maid tries to unravel a string of pantomime sausages. She frowns and looks perplexed, the sausages looped on her neck. A fourth maid enters the kitchen with an open newspaper in her hands. She is shouting. Her mouth keeps yawning and snapping shut. The other maids stop work and wipe their hands on their aprons. They swarm around the newspaper, stagger, swoon, cling to each other for support, their faces white with horror.

The German Invasion!

He stands in the shade of the shrubbery. He wears a cavalry uniform and a coal scuttle with a spike. His face is a skull in a fancy moustache. The Emperor of Germany! He draws a cape around himself and scowls through the bushes towards the house. Now he has shrunk to a shadow. The shadow flickers down the garden path and peeps through the kitchen window. A door opens and the shadow enters, creeps through a narrow corridor. No one suspects! The shadow tiptoes up the stairs, sweeping forward, plunging the walls into darkness.

Lady Wagtail's Bedroom

The Kaiser enters the room and glances quickly around him. The room is richly furnished with carpets and curtains and potted palms. But where is Lady Wagtail? Here on a table are bottles and brushes. There on the bed are silk gloves and slippers. The Kaiser wipes his moustache. His eyes have turned into small, black slits. He slinks forward, climbs inside a wardrobe and closes the door behind him.

Lady Wagtail retires for the night

Lady Wagtail enters the room and gently closes the door. She unbuttons her gown to reveal a chemise and a pair of short, black stockings. Now she unpins her hair and lets it fall to her waist. She bends to the bed, folds down the sheet and slaps around the pillows. When she stretches and bends across the bed the chemise lifts away to reveal her legs, the swell of her thighs, the shine of her fat, white buttocks. The room grows dark and frames the quivering arse in a perfect keyhole of light.

Look out behind you!

The Kaiser leaps from the wardrobe and falls upon Lady Wagtail. One hand pulls back her head while the other claws at the silk chemise. Her breasts spill out. Her mouth pops open in surprise. He squeezes her breasts and laughs. The teats jump about in his hands like India-rubber balls. Lady Wagtail rears up in fright, jerks out her arms and throws off the demon assailant. The Kaiser takes a tumble, falls from the bed, collides with a chair and somersaults across a table.

Help! Help!

Lady Wagtail is screaming. Her little chemise has disappeared. Her fine black stockings have vanished. The Kaiser is creeping over the carpet, his hands stretched out to her throat. For a moment she cannot move, frozen with fright, her face contorted with terror. The Kaiser strikes. She turns around and throws herself at the window. She wriggles. She kicks. But she cannot escape. He tosses her down on the ruined bed, grabs her legs and gazes, hungrily, at her feet. He might be planning to eat her alive. Where to begin? He surveys this bountiful feast of flesh, from the tangled hair on her lovely head to the soles of her dainty feet. Yes! He bares his teeth at a row of toes and pulls them into his mouth.

The Household Cavalry!

The bedroom door bursts open and the maids crowd into the room. The Kaiser snarls and jumps from the bed. He turns to the window and bangs his fists on the glass. But the maids pull him down in a storm of pigtails, ribbons and nightgowns. They stick him with pokers and poke him with sticks until he is beaten as flat as the carpet.

The punishment fits the crime

The Kaiser is stripped of his uniform and tied securely to a chair. The fight is already knocked out of him. He looks old and small and sad. One eye is black. A chamber pot sits on his head. The maids march around him in triumph. They open their nightgowns, bare plump breasts and taunt the helpless prisoner. Lady Wagtail comes on parade, wearing the Kaiser's boots and helmet. Now she stands before the chair, turns her back on the Emperor, bends at the waist and waggles her backside in his face. The Kaiser struggles against his ropes, moaning and shaking his head. Lady Wagtail sticks out her tongue, slips a hand between her legs and briskly fingers her beard. And so, with the maids marching, the Kaiser cursing and Lady Wagtail wagging, a Union jack unrolls from above and falls to the stage like a curtain.

48

'I never saw anything like it,' the sculptor called Spinks confessed. 'I'd heard about it many times but, bless my soul, I never saw it!' He shivered and blew jets of steam through his teeth.

It was ten o'clock on a bitter morning, the puddles frozen and the lawns still white with frost. Fortified by a large breakfast, the company, led by Lord Hugo Prattle, was stamping along the shores of the lake. Prattle carried a shotgun in his arms and paused, now and then, to stare at the sky. Spinks walked beside Valentine Crane and Marsh had been set to work, pushing Swann around the grounds in a basket contraption on wheels. Despite all his protests, Kingdom Swann's legs had been examined and declared unfit to balance his bulk in the frost.

'She was a fine figure of a woman,' said Crane, slapping his hands, 'and she wasn't afraid to show it.'

'That was nothing,' said Prattle proudly. 'You should see some of them picture shows. Pansy Waters is my favourite. *Pansy Waters in Bath Time Bubbles.* By thunder, but she boils the blood!'

'A proper parade of beauty,' laughed Marsh, driving the chair through a flowerbed. 'What do you say Mr Swann?'

'What?' roared Swann, through a bandage of woollen muffler.

'The picture show!' shouted Marsh.

'I couldn't watch it. The light hurt my eyes,' wheezed Swann. 'Tomfoolery!' He sniffed and swung out his arms. He'd been given a pair of bright orange pigskin gloves that stuck from the sleeves of his coat like a pair of artificial hands.

'You can't have missed that posterior,' shouted Spinks. 'I do declare it was a posterior of Old Testament proportions.'

'I couldn't make head nor tail of it,' snapped Swann, scowling at the leather sausages protruding from the ends of his sleeves. 'It was all so much confusion.' But he had seen everything. Living pictures on the wall! The whole of creation shrunk very small and chased down a shaft of light. If art was a search for beauty and beauty the celebration of life, then here were machines with the power to manufacture it by the yard. The photograph was dead. Cinema had walked away with it. He was shocked and dismayed by the knowledge. Last night's little exhibition had been no more than a tuppenny peepshow. But it had been enough of a demonstration to convince him of its power in the world.

'I thought the effect was most comical,' said Valentine Crane. 'There's nothing more amusing than watching nude women cavorting. Whenever I have the money I like my studio full of them. I put on some music and set 'em dancing. I'm too old to paint 'em. So I just sit and look at 'em. And I don't know which I like better!' He honked with laughter, caught a bad cough and began to choke in the freezing air.

'Patriotic!' barked Prattle. 'It was very patriotic!'

'That's the stuff to serve the troops,' said Marsh, who was hoping to make a fortune by building a small, canvas cinema, robust enough to be used by the army.

'Poor buggers!' said Spinks. 'They need something out there to raise their spirits.'

'I blame the Germans,' said Prattle. 'It's disgraceful the way they conduct themselves. They ought to wage war like gentlemen.'

'They sank a hospital ship! Did you hear that? Thousands of sick and injured men, helpless as rabbits, and the murderers laughed as they watched 'em drown!' shouted Spinks.

'It's not a war,' said Crane, spitting an oyster into the grass. 'It's more like a deadly disease. A terrible plague sent down from heaven and made to lay waste the earth.'

'And it's spreading,' said Prattle. 'The whole damn world is marching to war.'

'The world is always going to war!' wheezed Swann. 'I can remember the Crimea and *that* was a nasty business.'

'But that was sixty years ago,' said Prattle.

'It never stops!' shouted Swann. 'After the Crimea the Indian Mutiny, the first Ashanti war, the Afghan war, the Zulu war, the first Boer war, the war in Egypt, the third Burmese war, the second Ashanti war, the last Boer war, we nearly went back to war with the Russians and now we're fighting the Kaiser...'

'A man is born to fight,' argued Marsh, pausing to wipe his nose on his sleeve. 'He's a predator. It's in his nature to want to engage in trials of strength. If it's worth four farthings it's always been worth a fight. Remember the Children of Israel,' he shouted down at Swann. 'They never did anything else but fight.'

'But the Germans are devils!' cried Spinks. 'They'll stop at nothing. They're killing innocent women and children.'

'The Zulu were killing women and children,' said Swann, banging his fists against his knees.

'That was only to be expected,' said Crane. 'You've got to make allowances when you're dealing with the heathen.'

'That's understood,' said Prattle. 'But your German is a white man. Good God, he's very nearly an Englishman!'

'That don't stop him sticking babies on the end of his bayonet,' said Valentine Crane as they tottered through the rhododendrons and back towards the safety of the house.

'And it don't stop his spraying our lads with poisonous gas,' agreed Prattle bitterly.

'The heathen might be a savage,' said Spinks, 'and he might want to cut out and eat your liver, but you know where you stand with your Zulu and your Fuzzy-Wuzzy. He stands his ground with his shield and his spear and when you shoot him he dies like a man.'

'I don't like it,' growled Prattle, slapping his gun as he watched the sky. 'It's turned very ugly. They've already killed my butler, two coachmen and a groom. They'll have to be stopped or we'll have no staff left to manage the house. It's time we taught them a lesson.'

'You'd think, with all the progress we've made, we could put a quick end to a dirty, little war,' grumbled Marsh. 'We should build machines to fight our battles. That's the answer. These days machines can do everything. Why, they even have machines that are built to build more machines. Imagine the power of an army riding to war in a fleet of flying dreadnoughts or guns that could sniff out the enemy, take aim and fire themselves.' He fell silent, dreaming of beautiful engines of war, armour-plated fortresses, mounted on wheels, belching fire and farting smoke, uncoiling into the enemy camp like glittering Chinese dragons.

'And who drives your infernal machines?' snorted Prattle. 'Who looks after 'em when their works break down or their wheels fall off and they blow themselves apart? You'll be asking next for an army made up of motor mechanics.'

'It will all be done by electricity,' said Marsh mildly.

'You can't find a better fighting machine than a regiment of cavalry,' said Prattle, shaking his head.

'I heard that some American is already building a death ray machine,' ventured Valentine Crane.

'That should put an end to 'em,' chuckled Spinks.

'How does it work?' shouted Prattle.

'Electrocution,' said Crane.

'That's what I told you,' said Marsh triumphantly. 'When you understand electricity you've the power to conquer the world.'

'I saw a picture in a magazine,' continued Crane. 'It's a huge copper cannon that fires a deadly electric beam strong enough to knock down an army. They say, when it's built, it will finish the war in a week. There's no defence against this machine. It can burn a hole through the side of a mountain.'

'Lucky the Huns don't have one,' said Swann.

'God would never allow such a thing!' laughed Prattle.

'He gave 'em the poison gas,' barked Swann but nobody was listening.

'Isn't that wonderful?' said Prattle. 'That's science! A machine that will put an end to war!' He raised the shotgun and squinted along the barrel. He squeezed the trigger. There was an ear-bursting report and, high above their heads, a crow exploded in the bright, cold air.

'Gotcha!' he roared and everyone laughed.

49

The next morning Spinks returned to London and Valentine Crane made the long journey home to Cromer. Once Prattle had helped his guests board their trains he took Marsh for a spin in the car. They packed a basket of brandy and cheeses, buttoned themselves into waterproof jackets and sped off into the lanes.

Swann woke up to a silent house. He'd been dreaming of Fletcher-Whitby and his days in the painter's studio. A woman rampant in polished armour, the smell of horses and turpentine. *A Feast at the Camp of Boadicea*. In the dream he'd been a young man, scaling the heights of the scaffolding with a paint-brush clenched in his teeth. When he woke up he was old. He dressed slowly, shuffled down to the library and settled himself in his favourite chair. The short excursion exhausted him. A maid lit the fire and brought him a bowl of porridge and treacle. He asked for a flask of coffee but the maid did not return. He spent the rest of the day in the chair, forgotten and neglected.

It was nearly dark when Prattle and Marsh presented themselves at the library door. The sound of their boots on the marble floor startled Swann from his slumber.

'We've found the *Hall of Earthly Delights!*' shouted Prattle, very jovial, when he saw Swann crouched in the chair.

'The *Naturalist's Paradise!*' cried Marsh.

They stood before Swann and grinned down on him, their faces bright with brandy and their hot breath black from strong cigars.

'And yet I've a notion there's something missing,' said Prattle, frowning and poking an ear.

'What's that?' smirked Marsh and he winked at Swann.

'A tribute to the architect,' said his lordship, throwing open his coat to embrace the fire. 'Look around you, sir, and feast on the loveliness of women. There's nothing like it in the world. This treasure house of beauty! No pleasure palace in Persia with paintings of women more ravishing, no pagan temple to be found in Rangoon with statues cut more exquisite. But where's a picture of the man who uncovered 'em? Show him to me, Mr Marsh, and let me kiss the hem of his photograph. Where's a glimpse of the face that successfully launched a thousand hips?'

'Nowhere!' cried Marsh looking very surprised.

'Nowhere!' roared Lord Hugo Prattle.

'He'd make a queer sight,' said Swann, 'rubbing shoulders with so many buttocks.'

'You're historical,' frowned Marsh, biting on his cigar. 'You're the last of the old masters.'

His lordship nodded his head in agreement. 'I hope you'll do me the honour, sir, of sitting for your picture. I've already taken the liberty of making arrangements with Marsh.'

'What?' shouted Swann. 'What?'

'He don't do it as a general rule,' beamed Prattle, wrapping an arm about Marsh. 'But I told him to find the equipment.'

'All the best,' announced Cromwell Marsh. 'Property of the British All-Star Vitascope Company.'

'You want my picture?' gasped Swann, clutching his beard in alarm.

'It would be a privilege, Mr Swann, although I trembles at the thought of it,' said Marsh. The old man had been good to him and, despite his new-found success, Marsh wasn't the sort to forget a friend. He was eager to pay his respects.

'The Swann Library,' said Prattle. 'Your picture hung in a place of honour. Your name in gold above the door.'

Kingdom Swann looked terrified. He shivered and turned his face to the fire. His hands trembled as he rubbed his knees.

'What's wrong?' said Prattle, feeling disappointed. He'd gone to a great deal of trouble in order to do him these honours.

'I never had my picture taken,' confessed Swann. 'I was always behind the keyhole.'

'It don't hurt,' chuckled Marsh.

'I don't know,' said Swann. 'I don't know.' He began to nervously pull on his nose.

'We'll have it finished before you know it,' said Marsh.

'If it's all the same to you, sir, I'd rather decline your invitation,' said Swann. But his protests were in vain.

'Take his arm and help him along,' said Prattle, turning to Marsh. 'It's a cold night and we can't keep the company waiting.'

They helped him to his feet and guided him from the library. They led him across a quadrangle of moonlit flagstones and through a low stone porch. They coaxed him up and down flights of stairs, along empty halls and narrow chambers, towards the east wing of the house. Swann was complaining and gasping for breath but they would not let him rest until they had climbed to the top of the stairs that led to the painted ballroom.

Cromwell Marsh drew open the doors. The ballroom was full of light. A colonnade of cast iron candelabra blazed and smoked the length of its walls. It was bright and hot and heavy with perfume.

At one end of the great hall a sweep of polished steps led to a circular platform built to balance an orchestra. The steps had been covered in silk carpets and richly embroidered materials. A quantity of muslin fell in a drift from the ceiling to form a canopy over the stage. And in the centre of the stage, surrounded by cushions and tasselled pillows, stood a red, lacquered chair the size of a mandarin's throne.

The housekeeper stood beside the throne. She wore nothing but a pair of evening gloves. Her hair was tied in a knot and her eyes were obscured by a mask made from parakeets' feathers. Her skin was very white and the only colour it possessed was in the crimson of her mouth and the rouge on her tiny nipples. She stood in silence beside the throne. In one arm she held an hourglass filled with grains of fine black sand. The other hand cradled a human skull.

Beneath the housekeeper the housemaids, laundry-maids, kitchen-maids, scullery-maids and maids-of-all-work were arranged in order of importance. They were also naked but for the satin evening gloves and exquisite feather masks. Some wore ivory beads at their throats and others had pearls in their hair. They were sprawled upon the steps of the stage as if in voluptuous narcolepsy.

The entire household had been gathered before the throne, except for the crippled gardeners who were locked away in their cottages, sleeping off a ration of rum; and the cooks who, dressed in their best bib and tucker, were bent at a huge stone hearth, savagely stoking the fire.

As the three men approached, one of the maids raised an indolent hand to beckon Kingdom Swann forward. Prattle retired to a comfortable chair. Marsh attended his equipment. The camera he had borrowed was small and light and made the studio Fallowfield look like a clumsy museum piece. He adjusted the camera on its stand and patiently waited for Swann to take his position on the stage.

Swann ascended through the ghostly spiral of sprites until he had reached the red, lacquered throne. And then the sound of engines filled the hall. The ceiling shook with a rumble of thunder.

50

'It's the invasion!' bellowed one of the cooks and made a kitchen-maid scream.

'Silence!' hissed Mrs Petersen and kicked the maid in the back of the neck. The maid squealed and smothered her face in her hands.

The noise of the engines grew louder, shook the stage and rattled the glass in the window frames.

Prattle ran to the window and anxiously stared through his own reflection. 'It must be an air raid!' he shouted and turned to rescue Swann from the stage. Marsh, looking sick, clung to his camera while the maids began to dress themselves in all the available carpets and cushions.

'What's happening?' croaked Swann but his voice was drowned in the uproar around him. He toppled from his throne and knocked the skull from the housekeeper's arm. He followed the skull as it bounced down the steps and rolled across the ballroom floor.

'Stop him!' bawled Prattle, surrounded by struggling chambermaids.

The cooks ran forward and tried to catch him but Swann wriggled free and was gone. He was blundering down the central staircase when Mrs Petersen caught up with him and took him back to his room.

'Take the children to the scullery,' he whispered. 'Go and tell Alice to hide them…'

'There is no danger, sir,' said Mrs Petersen softly.

She took him by the hand, this tall, masked woman in evening gloves, and he was too confused to resist. A small fire burned in the grate. A plate of biscuits beside the bed. She pushed him into a chair and told him to behave himself and stay in his room until the raiders had passed overhead and she could come back to collect him. Her breasts quivered. Her mouth was the colour of blood.

He waited until she had closed the door and, when she was gone, he was back on his feet and searching for the stairs to the front of the house. His lungs hurt. The cold night air filled his eyes with tears. He turned and followed a gravel path that would take him home to the library. He didn't know what was happening but he knew that he was frightened and wanted to return to his ghosts. He wanted to be with his shadow hoard, restored to the arms of his fabulous women. Psyche, Venus and Aphrodite. The women he had known and loved and the women he had loved and forgotten. He wanted to be restored. He wanted to go home.

As he ran the terrible engine of war shrieked and seemed to swoop down on him. When he looked up he saw the machine, as big as a battleship, hung in the sky above his head. It shook the tiles on the roof and made the chimney stacks tremble. Swann staggered back through the shrubbery, fell down and blinked at the moon.

The Zeppelin had left its moorings in Germany for a bombing raid on Dover. Caught in a squall above the Channel the ship had been thrown from its course, lifted high and driven west towards the hills of Purbeck. Now the titan thundered towards the lake, turned to starboard and drew a great circle in the sky, attracted by the ballroom lights.

Swann dragged himself into the library and turned the key in the lock. He tiptoed down the darkened hall, through the corridors of leather books and hid behind a chair.

There was a sudden commotion from the house, the maids screaming, Cromwell Marsh shouting, and then Prattle was running across the lawn with a shotgun in his hand. As the Zeppelin made its second approach he jerked back the gun and fired both barrels at its flanks.

Nothing happened. He couldn't understand it. He had expected fireworks. He had expected the monster to perish like a ha'penny birthday balloon. He threw down the gun and bellowed with rage, chased the airship over the lawn and threatened its crew with his fists.

No one saw the torpedo as it slipped from the cradle. It fell through the moonlight, wagging its tail and plunged through the library roof. There was a muffled roar and the library windows exploded.

Prattle sent for Marsh who was sent to summon the maids who ran away to dress and were sent to wake up the gardeners who were sent to search for buckets and pails which were brought to the house and inspected by Prattle who instructed them to be filled from the lake and emptied into the flames. And meanwhile the library burned to the ground.

The gallery collapsed. The cabinets were exploding like cannons, charged with hat pins, old shoes and buttons. All along the smoking shelves flames sprouted from the spines of books, blistered their bindings, fanned their pages, releasing millions of photographs that fluttered and shone in the turbulent air. Dipped in fire they caught alight, flew to the rafters, gathered like swarms of smouldering stars. And the old man ran about the library, snatching at the photographs as they burned in spirals around his head. He jumped and danced until the maelstrom swallowed him and then he laughed as his feet left the ground, his beard blew sparks and he shot out to heaven, carried aloft on a glittering pillar of flame and smoke.

Epilogue

Lord Hugo Prattle sits astride a prostrate mourner and tosses a sprig of snowdrops onto the lid of the casket.

'He lived for the love of women and women was the death of him,' he declares. 'His work has perished but the man will not be forgotten.'

Beneath him, gathered in the shadow of the granite block, Alice and Ethel hold hands and try not to weep. The admirable Mrs Beeton and several girls from the Villa Arcadia murmur their approval and shuffle their feet in the snow. Marsh removes his hat and stares forlornly across the lake.

'He'll always be remembered,' forecasts Mrs Beeton confidently. 'He was an artist.' She is wearing a black panther coat and a necklace of Whitby jet.

'They should have shown him more respect,' said Alice fiercely, glancing at Marsh.

Ethel sobs and buries her face in her mittens.

'He was a man born out of his times,' said Prattle. 'But once he's better understood the nation will do him the honours.'

'One day they'll write a book about him, I shouldn't be surprised,' says Marsh, who is cold and tired and already thinking of Pansy Waters and the work that is waiting in Cricklewood. The weather is bad and the trains are so slow. It's time he bought a new motor car.

'We'll come here every year to put snowdrops on his grave,' says Mrs Beeton as the little congregation turn away to the house with the promise of hot punch and toasted muffins.

Lord Hugo Prattle turns, one last time, to admire the cut of the polished casket and the circle of niveous bums. God rest you Kingdom Swann asleep in your borrowed monument. And then he climbs down and follows the party through the snow to the warmth and the lights of the house.

Behind him the seven marble mourners awake, and a crack, no bigger than a worm, wriggles from the palm of an outstretched hand. The snowdrops shiver and fall to the ground. The tomb starts sinking into the lake.

New from The Do-Not Press

Ray Lowry: INK
1 899344 21 7 – Metric demy-quarto paperback original, £9

A unique collection of strips, single frame cartoons and word-play from well-known rock 'n' roll cartoonist Lowry, drawn from a career spanning 30 years of contributions to periodicals as diverse as *Oz, The Observer, Punch, The Guardian, The Big Issue, The Times, The Face* and *NME*. Each section is introduced by the author, recognised as one of Britain's most original, trenchant and uncompromising satirists, and many contributions are original and unpublished.

Paul Charles: FOUNTAIN OF SORROW Bloodlines
1 899344 38 1 – demy 8vo casebound, £15.00
1 899344 39 X – B-format paperback original, £6.50

Third in the increasingly popular Detective Inspector Christy Kennedy mystery series, set in the fashionable Camden Town and Primrose Hill area of north London. Two men are killed in bizarre circumstances; is there a connection between their deaths and if so, what is it? It's up to DI Kennedy and his team to discover the truth and stop to a dangerous killer. The suspects are many and varied: a traditional jobbing criminal, a successful rock group manager, and the mysterious Miss Black Lipstick, to name but three. As BBC Radio's *Talking Music* programme avowed: "If you enjoy Morse, you'll enjoy Kennedy."

Jenny Fabian: A CHEMICAL ROMANCE
1 899344 42 X – B-format paperback original, £6.50

Jenny Fabian's first book, *Groupie* first appeared in 1969 and was republished last year to international acclaim ("Truly great late-20th century art. Buy it." *—NME*; "A brilliant period document" *—Sunday Times*). A roman à clef from 1971, *A Chemical Romance* concerns itself with the infamous celebrity status *Groupie* bestowed on Fabian. Expected to maintain the sex and drugs lifestyle she had proclaimed 'cool', she flits from bed to mattress to bed, travelling from London to Munich, New York, LA and finally to the hippy enclave of Ibiza, in an attempt to find some kind of meaning to her life. As *Time Out* said at the time: "Fabian's portraits are lightning silhouettes cut by a master with a very sharp pair of scissors." This is *the* novel of an exciting and currently much in-vogue era.

Miles Gibson: KINGDOM SWANN
1 899344 34 9 – B-format paperback, £6.50

Kingdom Swann, Victorian master of the epic nude painting turns to photography and finds himself recording the erotic fantasies of a generation through the eye of the camera. A disgraceful tale of murky morals and unbridled matrons in a world of Suffragettes, flying machines and the shadow of war.

"Gibson writes with a nervous versatility that is often very funny and never lacks a life of its own, speaking the language of our times as convincingly as aerosol graffiti" *—The Guardian*

New from The Do-Not Press

Miles Gibson: VINEGAR SOUP
1 899344 33 0 – B-format paperback, £6.50

Gilbert Firestone, fat and fifty, works in the kitchen of the Hercules Café and dreams of travel and adventure. When his wife drowns in a pan of soup he abandons the kitchen and takes his family to start a new life in a jungle hotel in Africa. But rain, pygmies and crazy chickens start to turn his dreams into nightmares. And then the enormous Charlotte arrives with her brothel on wheels. An epic romance of true love, travel and food...

"I was tremendously cheered to find a book as original and refreshing as this one. Required reading..." –The Literary Review

Ken Bruen: A WHITE ARREST Bloodlines
1 899344 41 1 – B-format paperback original, £6.50

Galway-born Ken Bruen's most accomplished and darkest crime noir novel to date is a police-procedural, but this is no well-ordered 87th Precinct romp. Centred around the corrupt and seedy worlds of Detective Sergeant Brant and Chief Inspector Roberts, A White Arrest concerns itself with the search for The Umpire, a cricket-obsessed serial killer that is wiping out the England team. And to add insult to injury a group of vigilantes appear to to doing the police's job for them by stringing up drug-dealers... and the police like it even less than the victims. This first novel in an original and thought provoking new series from the author of whom *Books in Ireland* said: "If Martin Amis was writing crime novels, this is what he would hope to write."

Maxim Jakubowski: THE STATE OF MONTANA
1 899344 43 8 half-C-format paperback original £5

Despite the title, as the novels opening line proclaims: 'Montana had never been to Montana". An unusual and erotic portrait of a woman from the "King of the erotic thriller" (*Crime Time* magazine).

Jerry Sykes (ed): MEAN TIME Bloodlines
1 899344 40 3 – B-format paperback original, £6.50

Sixteen original and thought-provoking stories for the Millennium from some of the finest crime writers from the USA and Britain, including **Ian Rankin** (current holder of the Crime Writers' Association Gold Dagger for Best Novel) **Ed Gorman, John Harvey, Lauren Henderson, Colin Bateman, Nicholas Blincoe, Paul Charles, Dennis Lehane, Maxim Jakubowski** and **John Foster**.

Geno Washington: THE BLOOD BROTHERS
ISBN 1 899344 44 6 – B-format paperback original, £6.50

Set in the recent past, this début adventure novel from celebrated '60s-soul superstar Geno Washington launches a Vietnam Vet into a series of dangerous dering-dos, that propel him from the jungles of South East Asia to the deserts of Mauritania. Told in fast-paced Afro-American LA street style, *The Blood Brothers* is a swaggering non-stop wham-bam of blood, guts, lust, love, lost friendships and betrayals.

MILES GIBSON

Dancing With Mermaids by Miles Gibson
ISBN 1 899344 25 X C-format paperback, £7

'Absolutely first rate. Absolutely wonderful' – Ray Bradbury

Strange things are afoot in the Dorset fishing town of Rams Horn.

Set close to the poisonous swamps at the mouth of the River Sheep, the town has been isolated from its neighbours for centuries. But mysterious events are unfolding... A seer who has waited for years for her drowned husband to reappear is haunted by demons, an African sailor arrives from the sea and takes refuge with a widow and her idiot daughter. Young boys plot sexual crimes and the doctor, unhinged by his desire for a woman he cannot have, turns to a medicine older than his own.

'An imaginative tour de force and a considerable stylistic achievement. When it comes to pulling one into a world of his own making, Gibson has few equals among his contemporaries.'
– *Time Out*

'A wild, poetic exhalation that sparkles and hoots and flies.'
– *The New Yorker*

'An extraordinary talent dances with perfect control
across hypnotic page.' – *Financial Times*

The Sandman by Miles Gibson
ISBN 1 899344 24 1 C-format paperback, £7

"I am the Sandman. I am the butcher in soft rubber gloves. I am the acrobat called death.
I am the fear in the dark. I am the gift of sleep…"

Growing up in a small hotel in a shabby seaside town, Mackerel Burton has no idea that he is to grow up to become a slick and ruthless serial killer. A lonely boy, he amuses himself by perfecting his conjuring tricks, but slowly the magic turns to a darker kind, and soon he finds himself stalking the streets of London in search of random and innocent victims. He has become The Sandman.

'A truly remarkable insight into the workings of a deranged mind: a vivid, extraordinarily powerful novel which will grip you to the end and which you'll long remember' – *Mystery & Thriller Guild*

'A horribly deft piece of work!" – Cosmopolitan

'Written by a virtuoso – it luxuriates in death with a Jacobean fervour' – *The Sydney Morning Herald*

'Confounds received notions of good taste – unspeakable acts are reported with an unwavering reasonableness essential to the comic impact and attesting to the deftness of Gibson's control.'
– *Times Literary Supplement*

JOHN B SPENCER

Tooth & Nail by John B Spencer

ISBN 1 899344 31 4 – C-format paperback original, £7

The long-awaited new *noir* thriller from the author of Perhaps She'll Die. A dark, Rackmanesque tale of avarice and malice-aforethought from one of Britain's most exciting and accomplished writers. "Spencer offers yet another demonstration that our crime writers can hold their own with the best of their American counterparts when it comes to snappy dialogue and criminal energy. Recommended." – Time Out

Perhaps She'll Die! by John B Spencer

ISBN 1 899344 14 4 – C-format paperback original, £5.99

Giles could never say 'no' to a woman... any woman. But when he tangled with Celeste, he made a mistake... A bad mistake.

Celeste was married to Harry, and Harry walked a dark side of the street that Giles – with his comfortable lifestyle and fashionable media job – could only imagine in his worst nightmares. And when Harry got involved in nightmares, people had a habit of getting hurt. Set against the boom and gloom of eighties Britain, Perhaps She'll Die! is classic *noir* with a centre as hard as toughened diamond.

Quake City by John B Spencer

ISBN 1 899344 02 0 – C-format paperback original, £5.99

The third novel to feature Charley Case, the hard-boiled investigator of a future that follows the 'Big One of Ninety-Seven' – the quake that literally rips California apart and makes LA an Island. "Classic Chandleresque private eye tale, jazzed up by being set in the future... but some things never change – PI Charley Case still has trouble with women and a trusty bottle of bourbon is always at hand. An entertaining addition to the private eye canon." – Mail on Sunday

BLOODLINES the cutting-edge crime and mystery imprint...

PAUL CHARLES

LAST BOAT TO CAMDEN TOWN by Paul Charles

Hardback: ISBN 1 899344 29 2 — C-format original, £15
Paperback: ISBN 1 899344 30 6 — C-format paperback, £7

The second enthralling Detective Inspector Christy Kennedy mystery. The body of Dr Edmund Godfrey Berry is discovered at the bottom of the Regent's Canal, in the heart of Kennedy's "patch" of Camden Town, north London. But the question is, Did he jump, or was he pushed? Last Boat to Camden Town combines Whodunnit? Howdunnit? and love story with Paul Charles' trademark unique-method-of-murder to produce one of the best detective stories of the year.

"If you enjoy Morse, you'll enjoy Kennedy" — Talking Music, BBC Radio 2

I Love The Sound of Breaking Glass by Paul Charles

ISBN 1 899344 16 0 — C-format paperback original, £7

First outing for Irish-born Detective Inspector Christy Kennedy whose beat is Camden Town, north London. Peter O'Browne, managing director of Camden Town Records, is missing. Is his disappearance connected with a mysterious fire that ravages his north London home? And just who was using his credit card in darkest Dorset?

Although up to his neck in other cases, Detective Inspector Christy Kennedy and his team investigate, plumbing the hidden depths of London's music industry, turning up murder, chart-rigging scams, blackmail and worse. *I Love The Sound of Breaking Glass* is a detective story with a difference. Part whodunnit, part howdunnit and part love story, it features a unique method of murder, a plot with more twists and turns than the road from Kingsmarkham to St Mary Mead. Paul Charles is one of Europe's best known music promoters and agents. In this, his stunning début, he reveals himself as master of the crime novel.

BLOODLINES the cutting-edge crime and mystery imprint...

Hellbent on Homicide by Gary Lovisi
ISBN 1 899344 18 7 — C-format paperback original, £7

"This isn't a first novel, this is a book written by a craftsman who learned his business from the masters, and in HELLBENT ON HOMICIDE, that education rings loud and long." —Eugene Izzi

1962, a sweet, innocent time in America... after McCarthy, before Vietnam. A time of peace and trust, when girls hitch-hiked without a care. But for an ice-hearted killer, a time of easy pickings. "A wonderful throwback to the glory days of hardboiled American crime fiction. In my considered literary judgement, if you pass up HELLBENT ON HOMICIDE, you're a stone chump." —Andrew Vachss

Brooklyn-based Gary Lovisi's powerhouse début novel is a major contribution to the hardboiled school, a roller-coaster of sex, violence and suspense, evocative of past masters like Jim Thompson, Carroll John Daly and Ross Macdonald.

Fresh Blood II edited by Mike Ripley & Maxim Jakubowski
ISBN 1 899 344 20 9 — C-format paperback original, £8.

Follow-up to the highly-acclaimed original volume (see below), featuring short stories from John Baker, Christopher Brookmyre, Ken Bruen, Carol Anne Davis, Christine Green, Lauren Henderson, Charles Higson, Maxim Jakubowski, Phil Lovesey, Mike Ripley, Iain Sinclair, John Tilsley, John Williams, and RD Wingfield (Inspector Frost)

Fresh Blood edited by Mike Ripley & Maxim Jakubowski
ISBN 1 899344 03 9 — C-format paperback original, £6.99

Featuring the cream of the British New Wave of crime writers including John Harvey, Mark Timlin, Chaz Brenchley, Russell James, Stella Duffy, Ian Rankin, Nicholas Blincoe, Joe Canzius, Denise Danks, John B Spencer, Graeme Gordon, and a previously unpublished extract from the late Derek Raymond. Includes an introduction from each author explaining their views on crime fiction in the '90s and a comprehensive foreword on the genre from Angel-creator, Mike Ripley.

Shrouded by Carol Anne Davis
ISBN 1 899344 17 9 — C-format paperback original, £7

Douglas likes women — quiet women; the kind he deals with at the mortuary where he works. Douglas meets Marjorie, unemployed, gaining weight and losing confidence. She talks and laughs a lot to cover up her shyness, but what Douglas really needs is a lover who'll stay still — deadly still. Driven by lust and fear, Douglas finds a way to make girls remain excitingly silent and inert. But then he is forced to blank out the details of their unplanned deaths.

Perhaps only Marjorie can fulfil his growing sexual hunger. If he could just get her into a state of limbo. Douglas studies his textbooks to find a way...

It's Not A Runner Bean by Mark Steel

ISBN 1 899344 12 8 — C-format paperback original, £5.99

'I've never liked Mark Steel and I thoroughly resent the high quality of this book.' — Jack Dee

The life of a Slightly Successful Comedian can include a night spent on bare floorboards next to a pyromaniac squatter in Newcastle, followed by a day in Chichester with someone so aristocratic, they speak without ever moving their lips.

From his standpoint behind the microphone, Mark Steel is in the perfect position to view all human existence. Which is why this book — like his act, broadcasts and series' — is opinionated, passionate, and extremely funny. It even gets around to explaining the line (screamed at him by an Eighties yuppy): 'It's not a runner bean...' — which is another story.

'Hugely funny...' — Time Out

'A terrific book. I have never read any other book about comedy written by someone with a sense of humour.' — Jeremy Hardy, Socialist Review.

Elvis – The Novel by Robert Graham, Keith Baty

ISBN 1 899344 19 5 — C-format paperback original, £7

'Quite simply, the greatest music book ever written' — Mick Mercer, Melody Maker

The everyday tale of an imaginary superstar eccentric. The Presley neither his fans nor anyone else knew. First-born of triplets, he came from the backwoods of Tennessee. Driven by a burning ambition to sing opera, Fate sidetracked him into creating Rock 'n' roll.

His classic movie, Driving A Sportscar Down To A Beach In Hawaii didn't win the Oscar he yearned for, but The Beatles revived his flagging spirits, and he stunned the world with a guest appearance in Batman.

Further shockingly momentous events have led him to the peaceful, contented lifestyle he enjoys today.

'Books like this are few and far between.' — Charles Shaar Murray, NME

The Users by Brian Case

ISBN 1 899344 05 5 — C-format paperback, £5.99

The welcome return of Brian Case's brilliantly original '60s cult classic.

'A remarkable debut' — Anthony Burgess

'Why Case's spiky first novel from 1968 should have languished for nearly thirty years without a reprint must be one of the enigmas of modern publishing. Mercilessly funny and swaggeringly self-conscious, it could almost be a template for an early Martin Amis.' — Sunday Times.

Also available from The Do-Not Press

Charlie's Choice: The First Charlie Muffin Omnibus by Brian Freemantle – *Charlie Muffin; Clap Hands, Here Comes Charlie; The Inscrutable Charlie Muffin*
ISBN 1 899344 26 8, C-format paperback, £9

Charlie Muffin is not everybody's idea of the ideal espionage agent. Dishevelled, cantankerous and disrespectful, he refuses to play by the Establishment's rules. Charlie's axiom is to screw anyone from anywhere to avoid it happening to him. But it's not long before he finds himself offered up as an unwilling sacrifice by a disgraced Department, desperate to win points in a ruthless Cold War. Now for the first time, the first three Charlie Muffin books are collected together in one volume. 'Charlie is a marvellous creation' – *Daily Mail*

Song of the Suburbs by Simon Skinner
ISBN 1 899 344 37 3 – B-format paperback original, £5

Born in a suburban English New Town and with a family constantly on the move (Essex to Kent to New York to the South of France to Surrey), who can wonder that Slim Manti feels rootless with a burning desire to take fun where he can find it? His solution is to keep on moving. And move he does: from girl to girl, town to town and country to country. He criss-crosses Europe looking for inspiration, circumnavigates America searching for a girl and drives to Tintagel for Arthur's Stone… Sometimes brutal, often hilarious, Song of the Suburbs is a Road Novel with a difference.

Head Injuries by Conrad Williams
ISBN 1 899 344 36 5 – B-format paperback original, £5

It's winter and the English seaside town of Morecambe is dead. David knows exactly how it feels. Empty for as long as he can remember, he depends too much on a past filled with the excitements of drink, drugs and cold sex. The friends that sustained him then – Helen and Seamus – are here now and together they aim to pinpoint the source of the violence that has suddenly exploded into their lives. Soon to be a major film.

The Long Snake Tattoo by Frank Downes
ISBN 1 899 344 35 7 – B-format paperback original, £5

Ted Hamilton's new job as night porter at the down-at-heel Eagle Hotel propels him into a world of seedy nocturnal goings-on and bizarre characters. These range from the pompous and near-efficient Mr Butterthwaite to bigoted old soldier Harry, via Claudia the harassed chambermaid and Alf Speed, a removals man with a penchant for uninvited naps in strange beds.
But then Ted begins to notice that something sinister is lurking beneath the surface

The Do-Not Press
Fiercely Independent Publishing

Keep in touch with what's happening at the cutting edge of independent British publishing.

Join The Do-Not Press Information Service and receive advance information of all our new titles, as well as news of events and launches in your area, and the occasional free gift and special offer.

Simply send your name and address to:
The Do-Not Press (Dept. KS)
PO Box 4215
London
SE23 2QD
or email us: thedonotpress@zoo.co.uk

There is no obligation to purchase and
no salesman will call.

Visit our regularly-updated web site:
http://www.thedonotpress.co.uk

Mail Order

All our titles are available from good bookshops, or (in case of difficulty) direct from The Do-Not Press at the address above. There is no charge for post and packing.
(NB: A postman may call.)